YA
Ewi

P9-DEU-596

The lost one (Daughters of the
moon, #6)

DAUGHTERS OF THE MOON

the
lost one

Also in the
DAUGHTERS OF THE MOON
series:

DAUGHTERS OF THE MOON

the
lost one

LYNNE EWING

HYPERION/NEW YORK

Copyright © 2001 by Lynne Ewing

Volo and the Volo colophon are trademarks of Disney Enterprises, Inc.
All rights reserved. No part of this book may be reproduced or transmitted in any
form or by any means, electronic or mechanical, including photocopying, recording, or
by any information storage and retrieval system, without written permission from the
publisher. For information address Volo Books, 114 Fifth Avenue,
New York, New York 10011-5690.

First Edition
5 7 9 10 8 6
Printed in the United States of America

Library of Congress Cataloging-in-Publication Data
Ewing, Lynne.
The lost one / Lynne Ewing.—1st ed.
p. cm. — (Daughters of the moon; #6)
Summary: After awakening with amnesia and an
overwhelming sense of danger, a teenager discovers
that she has the gift of telekinesis and a long-standing
war with the evil Followers of Atrox.
ISBN 0-7868-0707-5 (trade)
[1. Supernatural—Fiction. 2.Psychokinesis—Fiction. 3. Los Angeles (Calif.)—
Fiction.] I. Title.
PZ7.E965 Lo 2001
[Fic]—dc21
2001026790

Visit www.volobooks.com

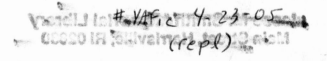

For
Amber Lee Fitzgerald

A scraping sound came from the kitchen below the little girl's bedroom. She wondered if her parents were still cleaning up from dinner. She glanced at the clock on her nightstand. It was four in the morning. At this hour they should be in bed, deep in slumber.

Another, softer noise made her tense. It wasn't the natural creak and pop she sometimes heard at night. Thump. The noise repeated. She sat up with a start. Someone was walking up the stairs. She threw back her covers, crept to her door, and peered into the hallway.

Her heart lurched. Two shadowy figures pressed against the wall. She could scream for her parents, but caution told her to be still. Instead she slipped back across her bedroom to her open window, pushed out the screen, and crawled onto the thick branch of an elm tree. She had done this many times. She liked to sit there to think and write in her journal.

She had never clambered the length of the branch to her parents' bedroom before, but it looked possible. She tugged at her nightgown and struggled to their window, then stretched her arms out to pull off their screen, but suddenly stopped.

The streetlamp cast a beam of light across their carpet. Why were they sleeping, sprawled together across the floor? She bit her tongue hard to keep the scream in her throat from coming out, then she blinked rapidly, not allowing herself tears. She needed her strength to find her sister, Jamie.

With new resolve she reached forward and tore off the screen. It fell to the ground below, landing silently in a bed of pink and red carnations.

She mounted the windowsill and pulled herself inside. She didn't let her mind consider what made the carpets warm and wet beneath her bare feet as she crept forward. She crouched behind their door and looked out.

The two men were entering her room now. As soon as they did, she dashed on tiptoe across the hallway to where her sister slept. She rushed in and almost tripped over Jamie, lifeless and curled in a ball near the canopied bed.

Her knees were suddenly too weak to hold her, and she sank to the floor, realizing everyone in her family was dead. She knew that soon the men would be looking for her. She rose and started to hide in the closet, but something stopped her. Instinct told her the two men would find her there.

Quietly she raced across the hallway and down the stairs, stooping low against the banister. When she reached the landing, she heard the men behind her. She swung open the door as their footfalls pounded down the steps.

At last she ran out into the night, guided by the full moon.

CHAPTER ONE

SUNLIGHT CREPT OVER her face and she jerked awake, thinking the enemy had been shining the beam of a flashlight over her. She sat up, body tense, and searched for the danger. At first she thought it had only been a nightmare that had frightened her, but then she knew something was desperately wrong. She didn't know where she was.

She glanced frantically around the small, one-room apartment. A refrigerator hummed in the corner, but she was confident she had never seen it before. Water dripped into a sink near the only window. Not one dirty cup, spoon, or plate sat on the spare counter, and no plants gathered the sun's rays on the windowsill. There was nothing she could recognize as belonging to her.

A lone dresser leaned against the wall near the door. The top was bare, polished and reflecting sunshine. An oak table with two chairs sat in the middle of the floor, but there were no pictures or personal items anywhere. Everything looked stark and freshly cleaned, as if someone had tried hard to erase all traces of the people who had lived here before. Then she spied a blue backpack leaning against the door. It had to belong to her, but it didn't look familiar. Nothing sparked any feeling of recognition.

She pressed her fingers against her temples, trying to recall what had happened the night before, but her mind was like a huge void. She couldn't remember how she had gotten into the apartment or when she had arrived. The bed had not been turned down. She had slept on top of the thin bedspread and was still dressed in jeans and a leather jacket. The hems of her pantlegs were frayed and black with dirt, her socks worn. She glanced at her rhinestone-studded tee. It seemed like something she'd wear to a party.

A pair of knee-high slick black boots lay scattered on the floor. She swung her legs over the side of the bed to put them on, and when she did, a large rusted pipe slipped from her lap and hit the yellow linoleum floor with a loud clank. She gasped as if it had been a snake, then slowly bent over and picked it up. Her hands began to tremble. Why had she slept with a pipe? Perhaps she had felt in need of protection. The cold metal felt lethal enough to crush a skull. Her chest tightened, and she wondered how such a brutal thought could come to her.

She tried to calm herself, taking long, slow breaths, but the air in the closed room was stale and antiseptic, making her feel even more claustrophobic. She needed to leave before it was too late. She had no idea where this strange impulse came from, but the urgency she felt was strong and growing. She glanced at her wrist. She had no watch and saw no clock in the room. From the bars of sunlight slanting through the window, she was sure it was morning.

Somewhere in the building a door slammed and she jumped. Only then did she realize how terrified she felt. Yet she couldn't understand why. She was alone. The room looked safe. But a bizarre tension shimmered around her as if someone or something threatening were present but not yet seen.

She closed her eyes, trying to bring back a memory from her past, and opened them again with a jolt of pure panic as realization struck. She didn't know who she was. She couldn't remember her name, her date of birth, where she lived, or who her parents were. As hard as she tried, nothing about her life before this moment came back to her. She glanced at the calendar hanging on the gray-green wall. It said November, but she didn't know the date.

Now instinct took over. The need to run was overwhelming. She glanced at the window as if she expected to see a threatening face staring back at her.

"Always trust your instinct," she mumbled, and stopped. The sound of her own voice startled her. It could have been that of a stranger talking to her.

She grabbed the boots, fell back on the edge of the bed and tugged them on, then stood. She had started walking toward the door when she felt something like a pebble under her right toe. She slumped onto one of the small wooden chairs, yanked off the boot, and shook out a soiled and crumpled note.

She unfolded it and read:

Dear LAPD,

It wasn't my imagination. Two guys were trying to kill me. If you're reading this, then they did. Now will you stop them?

Tianna Moore

A chill rushed through her and her body began to shake violently. Was she Tianna Moore? How could she be? It was like reading a name in the newspaper. It didn't feel like it belonged to her. She unzipped the backpack propped against the door, pulled out a notepad and pen, sat back at the table, and wrote *Tianna Moore*.

Her handwriting matched the writing on the note. Why would anyone want her dead? She couldn't have placed it in the toe of her boot recently. The paper looked old and stained. How long had it been there? A week? Two? Who was she running from? And if someone was trying to kill her, then why weren't the police willing to help? She should be able to remember something as important as that. She read the note again, then pulled on the boot, stood, stuffed the note in her pocket, grabbed the backpack, and rushed out the door.

In the hallway the smells of morning coffee, bacon, and burning toast made her stomach pinch with hunger. She wondered how long it had been since she had eaten. She felt starved. She rumbled down the stairs.

Her hand was on the front doorknob when someone called after her. Tianna let out a small cry and spun around.

CHAPTER TWO

"**G**OOD MORNING," THE voice called
again. "I didn't mean to startle you."

Tianna turned cautiously. An old woman
stood in the sunlight at the top of the stairs. She
started down the steps, clutching the handles of
two shopping bags. The bristles from a toilet
bowl brush peeked over the top of one.

"I'm Hanna," the woman said, as if that
should mean something to Tianna. She looked
safe enough.

"Hi, I'm . . ." Tianna paused and cleared her
throat. "Tianna." The name felt alien on her

tongue. She pressed her back against the metal mailboxes and stifled the need to bolt and run. Maybe she could gain some useful information from Hanna. Anything would help. She didn't even know what city she was in.

"I haven't seen you here before." Hanna came sideways down the stairs as if she had pain in her hips and knees. Her movements were heavy and slow. "Did you just move in?"

Tianna didn't know what to reply. "Yeah," she muttered, and played with the strap on her backpack.

"Usually I meet the new tenants right away." Hanna had a big smile. Her teeth looked plastic, and when she stopped smiling, her lips worked as if forcing her false teeth back into place. "I try to make this a happy place to live. Knowing your neighbors is one way to prevent crime."

Tianna looked at the front door nervously. The urge to run was consuming her, and she wished now she hadn't stopped to talk to Hanna.

"There." Hanna grinned when she reached the landing, as if getting down the stairs were a major feat. She set down one bag and extended her hand.

After a second's hesitation Tianna took it. The knuckles felt like cold marbles, the skin slick and thin.

"Are you all right?" Hanna asked with concern. Her breath still smelled of morning coffee, and it made Tianna's stomach growl.

"Why?" Tianna's voice sounded on edge.

"Your hands are wet and you look pale." Hanna picked up her bags. "I bet it's because you didn't eat breakfast. You always should, you know."

"Yeah, but we can't always." Tianna brushed a hand through her hair. "I didn't sleep well last night."

"Who does anymore? Police sirens all night long." Hanna started toward the door. "I'm just on my way to work. Need a ride?"

"Why would I need a ride?" Tianna asked.

"You missed your bus." Hanna stepped outside.

"I did?" Tianna followed her onto the stoop,

eager to know more. The morning sun was hot already and felt good on her face.

Hanna nodded. "I heard the bus go by a few minutes ago. I'll drop you at La Brea High."

"How do you know I go there?"

Hanna turned and smiled with half her face. "You don't look like you go to one of those private schools over on the west side." She stared pointedly at the frayed jeans and soiled backpack. "All the other kids in the neighborhood take the city bus to La Brea High, so it stands to reason that you would, too."

Tianna considered this with rising hope. "Thanks, I could use the ride." She readjusted her backpack, feeling suddenly reassured. She'd go to school, find her friends, and get some answers. Maybe she had been slipped some designer drug at a party the night before. She didn't know how she would know anything about designer drugs, when she couldn't even remember the last time she had eaten, but the information was there, easy to pluck from her brain. She wished other things would come back as readily.

Hanna headed toward an old gold Cadillac with huge fins and tons of dented chrome. The windows were rolled down and the cracked leather seats inside had gathered the morning dew.

"The windows haven't worked in ages," Hanna explained. "And it costs too much to repair them, but the old Caddy gets the job done; she'll get us where we want to go."

Tianna glanced at the California license plates. "You buy the car here?" she asked.

"Sure did," Hanna answered. "Right here in L.A. in 1966."

That answered one question at least.

While Hanna took a rag from her shopping bag and wiped down the car seats, Tianna surveyed the neighborhood. Old stucco apartment buildings and massive trees stood on either side of the road. Cars lined the curbs, and bicycles were chained to porch railings. Nothing looked dangerous, but she couldn't cast off the ominous feeling that something was lurking in the bright sunlight, unseen.

"What does your mother do?" Hanna asked as she folded the rag.

The question caught Tianna by surprise, and she turned back. "She's a dental hygienist," she answered with the first thing that came to mind, then paused, wondering if she was.

"That sounds like something that will come in handy in our apartment building." Hanna opened the car door.

Tianna looked at her sharply to see if she was teasing. She didn't seem to be. "Why?"

"Not many people where we live can afford to go to a dentist." Hanna nodded. "Get in."

Tianna swung her backpack onto the floor under the glove compartment. It landed with a thunk, and the dashboard rattled. "Sorry," she offered, then slid in and slammed the door.

"What do you have in that backpack, anyway?" Hanna asked.

"I don't know—" she began, and caught herself. "Books, things." She'd have to be more careful with the answers she gave or people were going to think there was something seriously wrong with her.

Hanna only laughed. "I know what you mean—when I clean out my purse, there's no telling what I'll find inside."

Tianna lifted the backpack onto her lap and unzipped it. Maybe she would find something inside that would help her remember.

The Cadillac pulled away from the curb with a belch of black exhaust, and a faint odor of gasoline filled the interior.

First Tianna found a tube of toothpaste and gratefully squeezed a long line into her mouth, then used her finger to brush her teeth.

Hanna glanced at her, then away. "A dental hygienist, huh?" she muttered, then laughed. "Did your mother teach you that?"

Tianna shook her head. Her mouth filled with toothpaste foam.

"Funny, I haven't seen your mother around," Hanna continued. "I know everyone. How long have you lived in the apartment?"

Tianna was stunned. How long? She didn't

know. She wasn't even sure that was where she lived. She leaned out the window and spit.

"Stop," Hanna said. "It'll come back in the car."

Tianna jerked around. A glob of toothpaste foam landed on the backseat.

"Sorry." Tianna leaned over and wiped at the white mess with papers she found in her backpack.

"Put your seat belt on!" Hanna bellowed. "You want me to get a ticket? It's against the law not to have your seat belt on."

Tianna hunkered down, making a mental note not to accept morning rides from strangers anymore.

Hanna glanced over her shoulder. "It'll come out. Sorry I yelled." But her voice still sounded perturbed. She concentrated on the road ahead.

That was fine with Tianna. She dug through her backpack and pulled out three pairs of panties. She looked at them strangely.

So did Hanna. "Do you normally take your underwear to school?"

Tianna felt baffled, and then her hand reached in and took out a bra, socks, T-shirt, and pj's.

Hanna laughed. "Are you sure you didn't grab a bag of laundry? What else do you have in there? It's like you're packed for a trip."

Tianna took out three textbooks, a stack of papers, and a wallet. Her heart pounded as she opened the wallet and looked inside. She didn't know what she had hoped to find, but it only contained three twenty-dollar bills. The significance of what was happening finally came over her. How was she going to survive? Perhaps she should go to the police again. Surely a detective could help her this time since she couldn't even remember who she was. But another worry flooded through her. Maybe whoever wanted to kill her would be waiting for her to show up there. Somehow it didn't feel safe.

Tianna turned over the paper she had used to clean up the toothpaste foam. It was her class schedule. "What day is it?" she asked.

Hanna glanced at her. "Wednesday. You

sound as old as me. Don't you even know the day?"

"No, the date," Tianna asked impatiently. "What's the date?"

"The seventh." Hanna looked at her curiously. "Did you mess up on your homework?"

Tianna shrugged and stared at the class schedule. She had enrolled on Monday the fifth. She had only been going to the school for two days. This would be her third. Where had she lived before the fifth of November? Now her plan to find friends and have them explain what was going on wasn't going to work. She probably had only met a few people, anyway. Tears pressed into her eyes, and she quickly brushed them away. She didn't have time for an indulgence like crying.

"What?" Hanna asked. "Is something wrong?"

"Why should it be?" Tianna snapped, and sniffed.

"No, it's just, you looked . . ." She shrugged. "Scared."

"Scared?" That wasn't what Tianna had expected her to say.

"Here we are." Hanna pulled to the side of the road.

The school was huge and crowded. Kids stood on the concrete steps and more leaned against the chain-link fence while others lounged around the trees. A guy with red hair seemed to be waving at her. She wondered if she knew him.

"Well," Hanna muttered. "It's a sad day when schools have to look like armed camps."

Tianna followed her gaze. Security guards stood at the front gate, checking purses and backpacks before kids stepped through a metal detector. A large sign hung near the entrance, explaining the penalty for bringing a gun to school.

"Thanks for the ride." Tianna got out and slammed the door.

Hanna honked and pulled away. Tianna waved absently and started walking to the gate.

Guys turned and eyed her boldly, some of their eyes lingering longer than they should. Even girls looked her up and down. It seemed like more than the normal once-over. She glared back at them with unwavering eyes. She wasn't going to be intimidated by a bunch of kids she didn't even know, especially when she had real things to fear. She glanced down the street. The air around her felt unnaturally heavy and filled with dangerous promise. Instinct told her she needed to hide.

She stopped near the end of the line and watched the way the security guards were ransacking the backpacks and purses. She didn't want them fumbling through her stuff and accidentally pulling out her underwear. She didn't have time for this nonsense, anyway. She kept her head down and walked to the front of the line.

When a guard turned his back, she slipped around the metal detectors and ran across the blacktop toward the buildings. Kids applauded her audacity. She didn't even stop when a guard yelled after her. His footfalls followed for a moment, then fell away. Just as she had figured, he couldn't chase after her. He had to get back and examine the long line of kids waiting to enter school. She hurried around a corner, and someone grabbed her shoulder.

"Jeez—" The word whistled out of her.

"Startled you, sorry." It was the same guy with the long red hair. He leaned close to her as if he had known her for a long time. His deep blue eyes were piercing, and he had a scattering of freckles across his long, even nose. "You want to go hang out in the computer room?"

"No," she answered, and made a face. She might not have her memories back, but she wasn't going to trade sunshine for a dusky room and a glowing screen. Then she smelled coffee and looked down at his hands. He held a huge blueberry muffin and a paper cup of Starbucks coffee.

She considered. What did she have to lose? "Give me a sip," she said.

He smiled and handed over the cup. She held out her hand as she swallowed the sweetened brew and he passed her the muffin. She took a huge bite.

"This is the best I've ever tasted." She wondered if it were true. She didn't really care. She took another sip and this time let the warm coffee linger in her mouth.

"You can have it all if you want." He seemed to be laughing at her. "Didn't you eat breakfast at home?"

"No time," she muttered. "And thanks. This is heaven—sunshine, coffee, and muffin."

"You're so different from everyone else," he teased.

"How so?" she asked, and took another eager bite.

"Other girls are so worried about the way they look."

"What?" She sprayed out part of the muffin and coffee. "What's wrong with the way I look?"

"Nothing," he answered, but there was amusement in his eyes. "You look great."

She handed back the muffin and the coffee, wiping her mouth with the back of her hand. "Then why did you say I don't worry about the way I look?"

"I just mean other girls spend hours in front of the mirror and you obviously don't. You seem like the right kind of person to go on adventures with," he answered in a dreamy kind of way.

"That's what I want to do. Go on a dig, maybe. Wouldn't you like to uncover mummies or discover an unknown temple in the jungles of Cambodia?"

"Why?" she asked with a rising sense of uneasiness. "When you're safe and at home, adventures might seem like fun, but when you're living them, they're not."

"I thought you'd enjoy roughing it," he explained. "You don't seem to care about appearances."

He had said it again. What was wrong with the way she looked? Then a sudden thought came to her. Maybe that's why everyone had been staring at her. She hadn't looked in a mirror, and Hanna wasn't likely to tell her anything was wrong. Old people always thought young people looked cute. Perhaps the other students were staring at her because she looked awful.

"What's wrong?" he asked.

"Where's a rest room?" Her eyes were already scanning the buildings around her, looking for a sign.

"Over there." He seemed confused. "Don't you remember where the rest rooms are?"

"Is that really important?" she snapped, grabbed up her backpack and ran. She slammed through the rest room door and skidded to a stop in front of the mirror, expecting to see black mascara rings under her eyes and lipstick smeared to her ears or, worse, a long smudge of dirt or snot.

She let out a loud gasp.

Three girls sharing a cigarette in a stall turned and gawked at her. The girl standing next to her stopped brushing her long, sun-streaked hair.

Tianna gingerly touched her eyes, nose, and lips. She was startlingly beautiful.

"Wow," she whispered, and brushed her fingers through her long silky black hair. Not many people ever got to see themselves as a stranger would. There was no prejudice in her vision or modesty imposed from a lifetime of living with her face and body. She could honestly say she was stunning. No wonder the guys were turning their heads, and the girls, too. She was a knockout.

The girl standing next to her began to giggle.

"What's your problem?" Tianna glared at her.

The girl stopped laughing, picked up her lipstick and hairbrush and started to back away.

"Wait," Tianna called to the girl who was slinking away from her.

She stopped and tentatively looked back, her finger nervously stroking her dangling earring.

Tianna tilted her head and smiled. "I need some makeup. Do you have any I can borrow?" Silly question, she thought. The girl's eyes were caked with purple shadow and edged with a harsh black stroke, lips outlined in brown and glowing with too much gloss, and her cheeks were brilliant shocks of color. She looked like she owned enough makeup to paint graffiti on a stadium wall.

The girl nodded and pulled a large blue case from her oversized purse. "My mother says it's unsanitary to share makeup," she said, trying to argue. She seemed intimidated by Tianna.

Tianna gave her a friendly glance. "Do I look like I could give you anything?"

The girl considered, then handed over her makeup bag.

"What's your name?" Tianna asked as she drew black liquid eyeliner over the top lid of her beautiful eyes.

"Corrine," the girl answered, looking at her oddly. "I sit next to you in geometry."

Tianna turned her head and stared at the girl. There was nothing familiar about her. "We must be friends, then," Tianna mused as she added dusky shadow.

The girl raised one eyebrow. "I'd like to be, but . . ."

"But what?" Tianna rolled thick mascara on her lashes.

"You didn't seem to like me," Corrine answered.

Tianna wondered how she had acted on Monday and Tuesday. Corrine seemed afraid of her. She held out her hand for the hairbrush. Corrine handed it over.

"You know . . ." Tianna spoke as she brushed her hair. "I was just in a bad mood.

New school and all. I'd really like to be your friend."

"You would?" Corrine couldn't hide her surprise. "Yeah, starting a new school is tough, but you seemed to be having it pretty easy."

"Me?" Tianna handed back the brush and added gloss to her pouty lips.

"I mean, every guy has a major crush on you." Corrine dropped the brush into her purse.

"You think that makes life easy?"

"I guess." Corrine stared at her. "I like the way you look. I've never seen you bother with makeup before."

Tianna considered what she was saying. She was confident that normally she didn't wear makeup, but today was a celebration. She was seeing her face again for the first time.

"You look beautiful." Corrine sighed.

"You could, too," Tianna scolded, then tried to soften her voice. Why did she sound so on edge?

"I could?" Corrine seemed eager for more.

"You've got great style," Tianna complimented

her, and it was true. She wore a pale green top, jeans skirt, and incredible side-laced boots. "But you look like a doll with so much makeup. I mean, you're so vamped out. I bet you look better with bare cheeks, and definitely ditch the purple shadow."

"Take some off?" Corrine reached for a paper towel.

"Yeah, it makes you look desperate and insecure," Tianna answered absently, and turned in front of the full-length mirror behind her. Her reflection thrilled her. "When's geometry?"

"First period." Corrine gave her a questioning look.

"Lead the way," Tianna ordered. "Let's go."

"Sure." Corrine gathered all her makeup and put on her sunglasses.

Tianna picked up her backpack and started out to the hallway with a confident swing in her hips.

A sly smile crossed her face this time when she saw the guys stare. She walked down the unfamiliar hallways next to Corrine. The knot of anxiety was beginning to unravel, and she started to relax. She felt a rising sense of security here. She looked up and down the crowded hallway. Maybe it was because she wasn't alone, not with a thousand other students pushing past her. It wasn't likely anyone was going to kill her here, not with so many witnesses.

She stopped suddenly and Corrine bumped into her. She needed to find out who would want to kill her and why.

"What?" Corrine asked.

"Sorry, mood swing," Tianna muttered, disheartened again. She closed her eyes, trying to recall the morning's panic. It had been hot and raw. Maybe if she was patient, by the end of the day she'd have a memory or at least remember who was after her and why.

"Over here." Corrine guided her.

They turned down an outside corridor. When they passed room 103, four guys dressed like skaters ran to the doorway and leaned outside.

"Hey, Tianna," the first one shouted.

"Looking fine," the second one added.

"Thanks," she answered, and watched the other two admire her.

"I can't believe the impression you've already made with the guys." Corrine giggled and stopped in front of the closed door to a classroom.

Tianna slumped against the wall.

Corrine lifted her sunglasses. "You got that funny not-here stare."

Tianna leaned closer to her. "Sorry, I was drifting." Then she noticed three girls standing together in the sunlight staring at her. "What's up with them?"

That made Corrine laugh. "You act so casual about it. I don't even believe you."

"Casual about what?"

"Everyone's talking about it. I'm sure they're just jealous. Usually Jimena, Serena, and Vanessa get all the attention, but you were the one who all the guys wanted to dance with last night. So why did you leave so early, anyhow? Nothing could have pulled me away from all that."

Tianna raised an eyebrow.

"You didn't!" Corrine squealed.

"What?" Tianna didn't understand.

"Leave with some guy," Corrine gasped, already assuming that she had. "You left with Michael, didn't you?" she whispered quickly, and looked back at the three girls, who were still staring at Tianna. "No wonder they're glaring at you."

"I didn't," Tianna answered, but she didn't know for sure. Had she left with someone? That might explain what had happened to her last night, but it still couldn't explain the unnerving feeling of danger she'd had this morning or the note in her boot.

Tianna decided to tell Corrine everything. Maybe there was some way she could help. "Listen, I can't remember—"

Corrine squeezed her arm. "Look who's coming."

Tianna turned and caught the eye of an incredibly good-looking guy in a black long-sleeved shirt, Levi's, and a beaded necklace. She immediately liked his style.

"Hi, Tianna." He had a great smile and soft brown eyes.

"Hi," she answered back, loving the way he looked at her. She didn't know who he was but she was sure they had done more than talk. At least she hoped they had. She glanced at his sensual lips and bit her own. She wondered if she had ever been kissed, especially by him. She hoped she had, but without a memory it was impossible to know.

"I wanted to catch you before class." He ran a hand through his wild black hair as if talking to her made him nervous. She liked that she had that kind of effect on him. "I've been looking for you."

"You were?" she asked. Her stomach felt queasy and she took three quick breaths. She didn't mind this kind of nervousness.

"We missed you at Planet Bang last night." His hand rested over her head on the wall. She could feel the warmth of his body, and she wanted to slide her arms around his waist and hug him, right there in front of everyone.

"How so?" she asked, and considered. At

least now she knew she hadn't left early with him, whoever he was.

"You've got great moves—"

"Moves?" she interrupted. "What does that mean?"

He burst out laughing. She loved his laugh.

"Your dancing," he continued. "Everyone wanted to watch you some more, but you left so early." The bell rang, and he ran backward away from her as if he were reluctant to let her go. "See you, Tianna."

When he left, she turned to Corrine. "Who's that?"

Corrine opened her eyes wide. "Are you kidding? That's Michael Saratoga, and everyone is talking about the way you were trying to steal him from Vanessa."

"Who's Vanessa?"

"I don't believe you. She's only the most popular girl in the whole school." She pointed a finger at the girl in the middle of the three who were still watching Tianna closely. "Everyone knows Vanessa."

Vanessa had perfect skin, large blue eyes, and luxurious blond hair that curled over her shoulders.

"Are those extensions?" Tianna asked.

"All hers." Corrine sighed.

Vanessa was dressed in a funky white coat of fake fur that went down to her brown suede boots; underneath was a low-hanging party-girl skirt with two gold belts draped around her tan waist.

"Where'd she get the clothes? They're so cool." Tianna glanced self-consciously at her own jeans. The knees were soiled, and there was a long black mark on the side, as if she had skidded in dirt or oil.

"Her mom's a costume designer for the movies," Corrine confided.

Tianna felt a pang of jealousy—not for the clothes, but from the mention of Vanessa's mother. She wondered where hers was. Why hadn't she been with her this morning?

"What?" Corrine asked, as if sensing Tianna's emotions.

"Nothing." Tianna shook her head.

"Don't compare yourself to her if that's what you're doing. You're glamorous in your own way."

A man walked toward them carrying a briefcase. That had to be the teacher, Mr. Hall. He drew a handkerchief from his pocket and wiped his nose, then stuffed the hanky in a back pocket and took out keys to the classroom.

Everyone started toward the door.

"Who's that other girl with Vanessa?" Tianna asked. "The one with the teardrops tattooed under her eye?"

"That's Jimena." Corrine spoke in a lower voice. "Don't mess with her. Everyone says she's been in a camp twice."

"Camp?" Tianna asked.

"Youth authority," Corrine muttered, as if Tianna ought to know. "I can't believe you didn't hear. It's all over school. She used to be in a gang."

"And the one staring daggers at me?"

"The one with the cello case is Serena," Corrine answered wistfully. "You should hear her play. I'm so jealous of her talent. She'll be famous someday."

Serena wore a fedora and a tie-dyed shirt with studded jeans. She had a beautiful face and compelling eyes.

"She also can tell your fortune with her tarot cards," Corrine whispered. "She read mine once, and it was spooky, everything she knew. I never went back for a second reading."

Corrine and Tianna edged closer to the door and joined the line forming to go inside the classroom. That's when she noticed that Serena, Jimena, and Vanessa each wore matching silver charms.

Corrine caught what she was staring at.

"They never take them off," she whispered. "Not in P.E., not for dances. Never. They had another friend, Catty, who wore the same amulet, but she's gone now. Someday when we're alone, I'll tell you what happened to her."

Tianna looked at the face of the moon etched in the metal on the charms. Sparkling in the morning light, the charms didn't seem silver but more like a strange stone that reflected a rainbow of colors. She glanced up to find Jimena staring at her, her black eyes intense, as if Tianna had done something wrong by looking at their charms.

She waited for the three to go inside, then spoke to Corrine. "Are they witches?"

"What?" Corrine asked, and her head shot around, eyes wide and frightened, then she glanced nervously back at the three girls.

Tianna was sure Corrine had heard her. She wondered why she seemed suddenly so afraid, but instead of repeating her question, she shrugged. She wasn't intimidated by them.

"Too bad for Vanessa," she whispered to Corrine. "I'm not going to let some old girlfriend stand in the way of my getting Michael."

"You are incredibly wicked," Corrine joked, and Tianna sensed the admiration in her voice.

CHAPTER THREE

AT THE END OF THE school day Tianna sat alone, writing her name over and over on a piece of paper, hoping to stir a memory. She had discovered very little about herself. Several times she had felt on the verge of recalling something, and then the feeling slid away. She could remember some things like the taste of coffee and potato chips, but she couldn't say what had been her favorite snack. Simple things like that had made her feel cut off from everyone else. It had been difficult to join in conversations, even though most of the kids had seemed friendly enough.

A hollowness filled her chest, and she pressed her fingers under her eyes. Crying wouldn't help, but even as she tried to push the tears away, her vision blurred.

She supposed that she should go back to the apartment where she had started this morning, but she didn't know how to get there. She had left in a rush, and instead of looking at the streets while Hanna drove, she had been rummaging through her backpack, searching for clues.

Her hands began to tremble again. She felt unsure. She had been vacillating between plans all day. Everything seemed too chancy. But that wasn't the worst part. The loneliness was. If she only had a parent or a close friend she could confide in, someone to comfort her and tell her that things would be okay.

The note she had found in the toe of her boot this morning had made her leery about going to the authorities, even the school vice principal. If the police wouldn't believe that someone was after her, then why should a teacher or principal? Maybe the best plan was to head for the Greyhound bus station in Hollywood and get out of town until she came up with some plan, but she was reluctant to leave. She felt safe here on the school grounds.

A shadow stretched over her, and she turned with a jerk.

Michael smiled down at her. He had taken off his shirt. Tattoos decorated his tan arms.

She wiped at her eyes carefully. She didn't want him to see the tears. And she definitely didn't want his pity.

"Hey, Tianna." His lips curled around perfect white teeth as he swung his backpack onto the table. He seemed happy to see her.

"Hi, Michael." She tried to keep the excitement from her voice, but already her heart was beating wildly. She wondered if he could tell how much she liked him.

"You okay?" He sat down next to her, and she caught the scent of spicy deodorant before he slipped on the long-sleeved black T-shirt.

"Sure," she said. "The sun was making my eyes water." She breathed deeply, disappointed that he had put on his shirt.

"I was trying to find you over at the gym." His dark eyes looked at her openly, and a pleasurable shiver raced through her.

She smiled, pleased that he had been looking for her, and studied his lips, imagining what they would feel like pressed against hers. Then with a shock of excitement she realized that she might already know if she could only remember.

"And why did you need to find me?" She leaned closer to him flirtatiously.

"I wanted to give you this." He dug into his backpack.

Eager anticipation flooded through her. She wondered if he had bought her a gift. A crystal, maybe, that she could hang on a silver chain, or a shell bracelet that matched his necklace.

He handed her a blue piece of paper. She took it and hoped he didn't see the disappointment on her face. "What's this?"

"My band's playing at Planet Bang on Thursday," he explained. "I hope you'll come listen to us. We don't go on until nine."

"Sure." She let a smile creep over her lips as she stared into his deep-set eyes. She had no idea where Planet Bang was, but she had been hearing kids talk about it all day and she knew if she went there, she'd be able to dance with Michael. She pictured his hands around her waist, his lips settling gently on hers. "I'll be there."

"You're a great dancer." Michael's body seemed to press closer to hers, and she wondered if he was doing it on purpose.

"I am?" she asked coyly, wanting to continue their conversation from this morning. Michael had watched her dance, but had that been while he was dancing with her? She liked the feel of his eyes on her, the way he was looking at her now.

"You know you are. You don't need for me to say it. You got enough compliments." The flyers fluttered in his hands.

"Your compliment is the one that matters." She let her finger stroke the top of his hand. He had the long fingers of a musician. She wanted to clasp his hand and bring those fingers to her cheek.

He smiled, teasing. "You want to hear more about how awesome you were?"

She wished she could remember what had happened. "Did you think I was?" She tilted her head and let her fingers trail up his hand, until all four entwined his wrist. She liked the warm feel of his skin beneath her palm, the rapid race of his pulse. She had a sudden desire to slide her fingers up his shoulder, circle her hands around his neck, and pull his face to hers.

"So how's everything going?" He stuffed the flyers into his backpack.

"Okay." How could she tell him that she had awakened this morning with no idea of who or where she was?

"It seems like something's bothering you." He watched her carefully.

She bit her lip. Did she dare tell him? It didn't seem right, but then, maybe he would have some idea of what to do. "Just things, you know."

"How could you feel down with every guy in school trying to hook up with you?" he asked.

She looked away. "A guy's not always the answer," she said with a sigh. "In fact, I don't think it ever is."

"All right, I said it wrong," Michael continued. "Have you met any guys yet that you think you could like?"

"I met you, Michael," she said softly.

"I'm talking about guys you might like, you know, for more than just a friend," he corrected her.

She eyed him slyly. "Why wouldn't I like you that way?"

He blushed beneath his dark tan and started to say something, but before he could, Vanessa ran up to them. She was wearing yellow baggy shorts, a white jersey, cleats, socks, and shin guards.

"Tianna," she called impatiently.

Tianna knew girls sometimes confronted each other over a guy, but this was ridiculous. She certainly wasn't going to have a shouting match with Vanessa in front of Michael. She stood and placed her hand possessively on his shoulder. "What do you want, Vanessa?"

But Vanessa didn't seem jealous. She didn't appear to notice the way Tianna's hand rubbed across Michael's back.

"Why aren't you over at the gym?" Vanessa raked back her thick blond hair and clasped it in a ponytail with a rubber band.

"Because I'm here." Tianna felt completely confused. This was definitely not the fight she had expected from Vanessa, but her answer made Michael laugh.

Vanessa shot Michael a warning look. He raised an eyebrow and stopped laughing.

Then Vanessa put her hands on her hips in frustration. "The soccer game is about to start."

Tianna looked at her dumbly. "So?"

"You're not even suited up," Vanessa continued, annoyance rising in her voice. "And we still have to do warm-ups."

Tianna didn't understand.

"You're my lead player." Vanessa seemed overwhelmed with frustration. "Come on."

Tianna choked. "How did I get on the soccer team so quickly?"

"Would you stop playing around? This is no joke. Decca High is our biggest rival, and I want to beat them." Vanessa was angry now. Her face flushed, and Tianna could see the vein in her neck throbbing. "Either you play or you don't." She turned and ran away.

"Come on." Michael took Tianna's hand. "We all want to watch you play, and Vanessa needs you."

Tianna bit her lip. How was she going to pull this one off? She wished now she had left school after the first bell. "I don't really think I'm going to help the team, and I sure don't understand what's got Vanessa so upset."

"Don't get too aggravated with Vanessa," Michael explained. "She gets crazy over soccer now. She and Catty used to play when they were little and she doesn't like to be reminded of it anymore."

Tianna looked up at him. She wanted to say "So?" sarcastically, but she had a feeling that there was something important in what he was trying to tell her. "Who's Catty?" she asked. "And what doesn't Vanessa like to be reminded of?"

He turned and looked at her. "You didn't know?" Michael had a curious expression on his face. "I thought Vanessa would have told you. That's the girl you're replacing on the team. She and Vanessa were best friends and then . . ." His voice drifted away.

"And then what?" Tianna needed to know.

"Catty went away," Michael explained.

"You mean ran away?"

"That's what I thought at first, but Vanessa insisted it wasn't so. Rumors started, but Vanessa won't really talk about it. She and her friends act like Catty's dead. So does Catty's mother."

"How do you know if they won't talk about it?" Tianna studied his face.

He leaned in closer as if he didn't want anyone to hear what he was going to say next. "I saw them putting flowers on the street a few blocks from Planet Bang as if they were making a *descanso*. It gave me the chills to watch them. I never told Vanessa that I saw them."

"What's a *descanso*?"

"It's where people mark the place where someone has died by laying down flowers and candles. Usually it's from a drive-by or a car accident." He looked up, and his eyes followed Vanessa as she disappeared inside the gym.

"You think she was killed and they're not telling anyone?" She had a sudden mental flash of the note she had found inside her boot. Maybe she wasn't the first one who had been chased down.

"If she was, a body was never found," Michael answered.

"That's terrible." Tianna suddenly felt sorry for Vanessa.

Michael shook his head. "You've got an important game to play." He seemed determined not to stay down. "You need to suit up."

"Are you going to watch me?" she asked.

"I wouldn't miss it for anything." He smiled down at her.

"Great," she answered with faked enthusiasm. She was going to be the joke of the school after this was over. Even if she strained, she couldn't remember how to play. Why had they put her on the team in the first place?

CHAPTER FOUR

TIANNA ENTERED THE gym, her boots scuffing on the cement floor. The steamy smells of damp towels and sweat confronted her as she looked down the long line of gray lockers. She didn't know which one was hers. She had cut P.E. earlier in the day for the same reason; it felt too embarrassing to ask someone to help her find her locker, and she wouldn't have remembered her combination, anyway. Besides, she hadn't been in the mood to play. She had spent the hour sitting in the warmth of the sun.

"Hola." The word echoed around her. She turned. Jimena sat on a bench, putting on her

shoes. She was wearing fluorescent blue shorts and a shirt; her long black hair was braided and stacked on her head.

"Aren't you and Vanessa on the same team?" Tianna asked, eyeing the uniform. She dropped her backpack and slouched beside her.

"I'm the goalie," Jimena answered, and pulled long white socks over her shin guards.

"And?" Tianna ran her finger over the graffiti scratched into the bench.

"Goalkeeper's uniforms don't match the team," Jimena explained impatiently. "You know that." Then she looked at her oddly. "Are you all right?"

"Of course I am," Tianna lied.

"Then why aren't you suited up?" Jimena rubbed sunblock on her face. "This is the big game."

"I can't remember my combination," Tianna confessed. She didn't bother to add that she also couldn't recall which locker belonged to her.

Jimena tossed the tube of sunscreen. It hit the back of her locker with a loud metallic clank.

She turned and gave Tianna a derisive grin.

"What?" Tianna asked.

"Just strange you can't remember your combination," Jimena retorted. "Because we have key locks here."

Tianna bit her lip. "Can you show me my locker, then? I can't remember which one is mine."

The scowl dropped from Jimena's face and she laughed with understanding. "Yeah, this school is really big. I was overwhelmed when I first transferred in, too. Don't worry about not remembering. I had to carry my class schedule with me for an entire week."

Tianna smiled gratefully and followed Jimena down the row of lockers. Jimena's cleats made a clicking sound on the floor.

"You were assigned Catty's old locker, right?" Jimena asked as she turned and they walked down another drab line of metal boxes.

"Right," Tianna answered, even though she had no idea if that was true.

Jimena stopped in front of a locker near a floor-length mirror.

"This one was Catty's," she said softly.

A watercolor painting of the full moon rising over an ocean was taped to the front. A beautiful woman hovered behind the moon, her purple robe billowing into the starry sky behind her. The image was haunting.

"Did she do the painting?" Tianna asked. "It's really pretty."

Jimena nodded. "She was a good artist."

"I guess the locker is a hard one to miss. I should have gone up and down the aisles until I found it," Tianna said, even though she knew she still wouldn't have been able to recognize it as belonging to her.

"That's okay," Jimena answered with a shrug, and continued staring at the picture as if she missed Catty a lot.

Then another problem occurred to Tianna. "Is my uniform inside, or do I get it from another place?"

Her question jerked Jimena from her reverie. "You forgot that, too? Vanessa gave you Catty's shirt and shorts. You're the same size. I hope you

◄   5 5   ►

kept them in your locker. You can't play without a uniform."

"What happened to Catty?" Tianna asked.

Jimena's mood changed abruptly, and Tianna knew she had trod in forbidden territory.

"Long story." Jimena tried to smile, but her look was more guarded now than friendly. "So I'll see you out on the field."

"Yeah." Tianna tossed her backpack on the bench, unzipped it, and started looking for a key.

Jimena turned back. "You don't have your key?" There was exasperation in her voice now.

"I have it," Tianna answered. "I just have to find it." At least she hoped she did.

"Hurry, then," Jimena answered, and turned to leave.

"I will." Tianna found a key chain with a couple dozen keys jangling from the ring. She stared at it, perplexed, and wondered what the keys were for.

"Why do you have so many keys?" Jimena asked, as if the same question had occurred to her.

Tianna shrugged. "Just things."

Jimena stepped back to her. "You don't remember which key?"

"I don't." Tianna tried the first key.

Jimena sat down beside her. "Are you doing this on purpose?" she asked. "The game with Decca High is really important."

"I'm doing my best," Tianna assured her, and pushed the next key into the padlock.

"I hope you're not trying to make the game start late." Jimena seemed dismayed. "We'll get penalized. *¿Sabes?*"

"I'm not trying to make us late," Tianna answered. "And if you're so worried about it, get a substitute."

"Engreída," Jimena muttered.

"What does that mean?" Tianna jerked around and glared at Jimena.

"It means you got a big head. You know we're counting on you for this game Maybe Vanessa will beg you to play, but I won't."

"Leave me alone," Tianna said, and the padlock snapped open. She unhooked the lock and pulled out a white jersey and yellow shorts that matched Vanessa's. She placed the shoes with cleats on the bench beside her, then took out a clean pair of socks, a sports bra, and shin guards. She wondered if all these had belonged to Catty or if she had purchased some of them. The shoes looked new. She stared at them in wonder but couldn't remember ever seeing them before.

"Warm-ups are starting," Jimena reminded her. "I'll see you out on the field."

"All right." Tianna took off her boots, then her jeans, stripped off her T-shirt and then her bra. She was about to put on the sports bra when she caught her naked reflection in the mirror.

It might as well have been the face of a stranger that stared back at her, but that wasn't what was bothering her. Her body was covered with bruises as if she had been in a major fight. A thick black knot the size of a shoe was bleeding a pale green color into her ribs, and another long red welt crossed her back as if someone had hit her with a stick. *Or a pipe.* She felt suddenly chilled, and her skin broke out with gooseflesh. How could she not remember such a brutal attack? And then another thought made her wonder. Why didn't the police believe that her attackers were real? Hadn't they seen the bruises? She touched another one on the top of her thigh. It felt hot beneath her fingers, and she wondered if she was getting an infection as well.

Maybe she had been mugged. She had heard of people getting amnesia from blows to the head. Where that information came from she couldn't say, but she knew it was true. That might also explain why she had such a strong feeling of impending danger. That would be natural after such a fierce attack, but it couldn't explain the note. Unless whoever had done this to her had been trying to do more than mug her. Her heart raced.

Something moved behind her, and she caught Jimena's reflection in the mirror.

"What are you staring at?" Tianna asked angrily as she grabbed the sports bra and tugged it on.

"You want to talk?" Jimena's voice was gentle now, and she sat down as if there was all the time in the world before the soccer match would begin. "I'm sorry for getting upset with you. I know what was going on in your head now."

"No, you don't." Tianna pulled on her socks, then the shoes.

"Who beat you up?" Jimena asked softly.

"I fell," Tianna answered curtly, and slipped the jersey over her head.

"You think I haven't seen what a kick to the ribs looks like the day after?" Jimena's hand reached out to comfort her, and Tianna jerked her shoulder away.

"I don't remember what happened to me," Tianna replied. "Just forget about it.

"Whatever you say stays here with me." She pointed to the two tears tattooed under her eye. "I won't go to the cops."

Tianna stepped into her shorts. "Like they could help, anyway."

"But maybe I can," Jimena offered.

"Right." Tianna started walking away. "I got enough problems. Just leave me alone."

She could hear Jimena's cleats clicking after her.

"What?" Tianna turned on her.

"You forgot your shin guards." Jimena handed them to her.

Tianna grabbed them. She sat on the nearest bench and put them on, hating the way Jimena hovered over her.

Finally she stood. "I don't want your pity," she said through clenched teeth. She grabbed up a ball and ran.

Outside, she set the ball on the ground and stared down at it. This was really bad. The game was going to be a total disaster if the team was in any way counting on her, and from what Jimena had said, she suspected that they were. She nudged the ball with the tip of her toe.

"Hey!" someone shouted.

She glanced up, and suddenly the guy with the red hair from this morning ran toward her. His foot kicked the ball, and he dribbled it away.

She had started after him when Vanessa yelled from the field, "Tianna, would you stop playing around? Bring the ball and get over here for warm-ups."

Tianna whipped around, ready to scream *I quit!* But then she saw Michael standing next to Vanessa. He waved at her, his big, gorgeous smile covering his dark, perfect face.

Tianna turned back to the guy. "Just give me the ball."

He grinned at her as if daring her to steal it back.

"Look, please." Tianna frowned, her anger growing. "Do you want Vanessa to get more upset with me than she already is?"

"You're her star player," he teased. "You can be late."

"Tianna," Vanessa called again. "If you don't get out here, I'm going to kick you off the team!"

"Like I care!" Tianna shouted back. Then she remembered Michael and how much he didn't want to upset Vanessa because she was still getting over the death of her friend Catty. "I mean, I'll be right there!"

She looked at the guy. Anger seethed inside her. "Give me that dumb ball. This has not been a good day, and I really can't take any more."

"Come get it, then." He smirked and ran away from her, kicking the ball lightly with the inside of his feet. He didn't look down, and he never lost control over it.

Tianna sighed and shook her head.

"Come on." He taunted her, and picked up speed. "You afraid you can't get it back from me?"

Something exploded inside her. She felt it like a hot fire flashing up to her face. She dashed after him and caught him in seconds. He seemed surprised by her speed but also delighted.

When she reached him, he darted away, changing direction, but it seemed as if her body had anticipated where he was going to go and she ran parallel with him, her feet tipping in and trying to steal the ball.

He laughed and shifted his weight in one direction, then took off running in the other, using the inside of his foot to roll the ball.

"Wrong thing to do," she shouted angrily. This time her feet went on automatic. She ran alongside him, then swung her leg in front of him and struck the near side of the ball. It popped away from him.

Her foot shot out again. He tripped and fell flat on his back.

She picked up the ball and sauntered back to him, then held out her hand to help him up.

"You don't have to smile so big," he said with a matching grin. He took her hand. His felt warm and strong.

She couldn't help but smile. No wonder they put her on the team so quickly. Her feet had talent. She was a master.

"Say, what's your name?" she asked as he stood.

He looked at her oddly but didn't let go of her hand. "Derek," he answered, and he seemed hurt. "You're teasing me, right?"

She didn't know his name, but suddenly there was no doubt in her mind that they had known each other before she lost her memories.

"Of course, I'm teasing," she lied, and ran out to the field.

CHAPTER FIVE

"¡*P*UENTA!" JIMENA SHOUTED, and dove for the ball. Her defenders cleared away and Jimena made another save. She punted the ball, and it went flying past midfield.

"Got it!" Tianna cried out. She threw out her arms and hit the ball with her forehead. It shot at the goal. The keeper tried to grab the ball, but it hit the net.

Jimena screamed, "Gooooaaaalll!"

Serena cupped her hands around her mouth and joined in from the sidelines. "Way to go,

Tianna!" Then she threw her hands over her head and gave a loud, "Woo-hoo!"

Tianna smiled at Michael, standing next to Serena and Derek.

"That was awesome!" Vanessa ran to Tianna and hugged her. "You're the best striker I've ever seen." She got a funny look on her face. Tianna wondered if she felt as if she was betraying Catty by saying that.

"Thanks." Tianna turned back as the goal-keeper threw the ball in a javelin pass. It hit her hard in the face.

"You did that on purpose," Vanessa yelled at the goalkeeper.

"Sorry," the girl called back. "It was an accident."

"I know you better than that, Michelle," Vanessa answered angrily. "You've done things like this before."

Tianna grabbed her nose and sat down on the grass, then leaned back and pinched hard, trying to stop the flow of blood. Her eyes teared; she felt sharp pain in her head.

Without warning a memory streaked across her mind, as if the impact of the ball had loosened something inside her skull. Someone dangerous wanted to destroy her, and it wasn't some ordinary pervert or stalker. The two guys who had been chasing her had feral eyes that glowed like a cat's in the dark. They also had mysterious powers of mind control.

"Tianna, are you all right?" Vanessa leaned over her.

She didn't answer. She was vaguely aware of the pounding feet of her teammates, running up to her, but she studied the memory. No wonder the police didn't believe her. She could barely believe it herself. Yet she knew it was true. She must have told the officers that her attackers had tried to hypnotize her with their glowing yellow eyes. She shuddered. How was that possible? She concentrated, but her mind gave her no more.

Vanessa knelt beside her. "Do you think she broke your nose?"

Tianna shook her head and looked at the blood on her hands.

"Oh, no, what have I done?" Michelle asked with mock sincerity. "I hope you don't have to sit out the game, Tianna."

"Not a chance," Tianna answered.

"That's not very nice, Michelle," Vanessa shot back.

"Especially since you did it on purpose," Jimena added.

"What do you mean?" Michelle asked innocently. "I'm just worried about her. Do you think I want you to lose your best player? I hate a game when there's no competition."

"Somebody get me a towel," Tianna said. "I want my penalty shot."

"No way." Michelle smirked and pulled her dark, curly hair away from her face. "I'm still in the game, and no one's called a foul."

"Tianna should get a free kick." Vanessa glanced over her head and waved for the referee.

"She got in my way," Michelle argued back. "I was only trying to get the ball down to midfield for the kickoff. Besides, even if the referee called a foul, which she didn't, you're not going to get another shot past me."

The referee walked over to them. "What is it?"

"Michelle threw the ball at Tianna on purpose," Vanessa said.

Michelle folded her arms across her chest. "She got in the way."

The referee looked at Michelle and shook her head. "I didn't see it," the referee said to Vanessa, then asked Tianna, "Can you still play?"

"Sure." Tianna nodded.

The referee didn't look convinced. "Your nose has to stop bleeding before I can let you back in the game."

"I'm fine." Tianna pinched her nose and glared at Michelle. "Nothing's going to keep me from playing."

"I'll get a towel." Vanessa hurried away.

The referee picked up the ball and started back to midfield as the other girls drifted back to their positions.

Michelle waited until everyone was far

enough away, then she leaned over Tianna. "Decca High hasn't lost a game all season," she said. "And we're not going to start with getting beaten by a loser team like La Brea High. It's not even fair that they let you play."

"What are you trying to say?" Tianna asked.

"What do you think?" Michelle sneered. "With you out of the game we're going to win. No way La Brea can beat us then." She turned and started to walk away.

"I hope you break an ankle," Tianna shouted after her.

"Fat chance." Michelle laughed, but then she tripped. She screamed and grabbed her ankle, then turned and looked back at Tianna accusingly. "You did that!"

"What?" Tianna asked, and spread her hands wide. "I was back here."

"You did something." Michelle searched the ground around her as if she were looking for the thing that had tripped her. "What did you do?"

"I didn't do anything." Tianna felt terrible.

She knew it was silly. A thought couldn't make something happen, but she couldn't squelch the guilty feeling that it was her fault Michelle had fallen.

CHAPTER SIX

THE REFEREE RAN back to them. "What happened now?"

"She tripped me," Michelle squealed.

"How could I?" Tianna said. "I was sitting here the whole time. She's ten feet away from me."

The referee looked from one girl to the other. "She couldn't have tripped you, Michelle; she hasn't moved since I was here before."

"But she did," Michelle protested, her forehead twisted in pain, and when she protectively placed her hands around her ankle, she let out a small moan.

Vanessa came back and gave Tianna a towel. "What's wrong?"

"Michelle fell and she thinks I did it." Tianna pressed the towel against her nose. It was still bleeding badly.

"You'd both better go to the nurse," the referee announced. "Tianna, can you help Michelle get there?"

"Yes," Tianna answered, not bothering to hide her disappointment at being unable to finish the game.

"I don't want her to touch me," Michelle yelled.

"Michelle, she couldn't have hurt you," the referee said. "She was lying on the ground."

Tianna stood, walked over to Michelle, and offered her a hand.

Michelle slapped it away. "Don't touch me."

"I'll get someone." Vanessa waved, and Derek and Michael ran onto the field. "Can you take Michelle to the school nurse?" she asked them.

"Sure," Michael answered, and cast a quick glance at Tianna. "Awesome play."

Derek and Michael locked their hands and carried Michelle to the nurse's office between them. Tianna followed, holding back her head.

At the nurse's office Derek lingered near the door. "You want me to stay?" he asked. "And give you a ride home?"

Tianna shook her head.

He gently moved the towel away from her face. "It doesn't even look swollen."

"But Michelle's ankle is," Michael said. "It looks really bad."

The nurse suddenly appeared at the door. She was a short, fat woman with a cropped pixie cut and happy gray eyes behind purple frames that were too large for her face. "Thank you for your help," she said. "Now, you boys go on so I can take care of the girls."

Tianna mouthed good-bye and reluctantly followed the nurse inside her office.

A few minutes later Tianna sat on a stool under a buzzing fluorescent light, holding an ice pack to her nose as the nurse examined Michelle's foot in the other room.

Tianna glanced idly around the nurse's office and stopped at the desk. The nurse had left her computer on and open to confidential school files. Her eyes shot back to the door to the examining room. The nurse was still busy with Michelle.

Cautiously she set down the bag of ice and crept over to the computer. She grabbed the mouse and scrolled down through the health files marked CONFIDENTIAL until she came to the one for Tianna Moore.

Her heart beat rapidly when she read her own name. She opened the file, then studied the information on the screen. Born 1986 in Los Angeles, California. Normal immunization records and illnesses. The last line surprised her. *Habitual runaway. Paranoid tendencies. Recommend counseling at Children's Hospital.*

Tianna read the last line again. Had she said something to the school nurse about being chased by strange men with glowing eyes?

Then she heard movement in the next room.

"I'll be right back," the nurse told Michelle. "I'm going to call your parents. You need to go to the hospital for X rays. I'm sure your ankle is broken."

"No!" Michelle moaned. "I'm the goalkeeper. How's my team going to play?"

Tianna had started to close down her file when something caught her attention. She saw her home address. She picked up a pen from the desk and hurriedly copied it onto her palm.

The nurse's shoes squeaked on the polished linoleum floor, coming closer now.

Quickly she grabbed the mouse, closed down her file, and turned away from the computer.

The nurse entered the room and eyed Tianna suspiciously. "Was there something you needed?" she asked, and scanned her desk, then looked at the computer screen. Tianna hadn't taken the screen back to where it had been before, but she hoped the nurse didn't remember what had been there.

"I think I'm okay to go home now if that's

all right with you." Tianna stepped away from the desk.

"Let's see." The nurse held either side of Tianna's head with gentle hands and moved it from side to side, then pushed it up and looked inside her nose again.

"All right," she said with an overworked smile. "But make sure you rest, or your nose will probably start bleeding again."

Tianna headed for the door.

"Wait." The nurse gave her four forms to take home and fill out and another one with instructions for her home care. "Read it carefully just in case."

Then Michelle yelled from the other room, "Has everyone forgotten about me?"

"I'm calling now," the nurse yelled back.

Outside in the hallway Tianna stared at the address written on her palm. That took care of one problem at least. She'd know how to get back to the apartment building. Maybe someone would be waiting for her, like a mom or a dad. Perhaps her parents had had to leave for work early this morning. It was comforting to think she wasn't alone.

She had started walking quickly back to the gym to pick up her backpack and change into street clothes when another thought alarmed her. The guys with the yellow burning eyes could also be waiting for her. She slowed her step. She had a sudden impulse to run, but she didn't know where to go.

CHAPTER SEVEN

THE LATE-AFTERNOON sun cast orange
light at a low angle and long black shadows swept
across the street. Tianna stared at the house in
front of her and compared its address to the one
written on her palm. The address was correct, but
this large brick Tudor home with its massive
chimney and steeply pitched roof was definitely
not the apartment building she had left earlier
this morning. She wondered if this was where she
lived. She studied the tall, narrow windows.
Perhaps one belonged to her bedroom.

She couldn't help but hope her parents were

inside. Maybe they had been desperately looking for her. Her heart pounded crazily as she unzipped her backpack and pulled out the chain with the dangling keys. Did she have the right one to get inside? She glanced back at the dark house. More than anything she wanted to be home and feel the comfort of a parent's arms around her.

She took a deep breath and hurried across the street, stepped up a short flight of stairs between two thick ornate iron banisters, then followed a brick path to the porch, where she skipped up the steps and rang the doorbell twice.

No one answered.

She hadn't really expected anyone would. Her hands trembled badly, making the keys jingle like wind chimes as she stuck the first one in the lock. The looseness of the doorknob surprised her. She tried one key, then another. Finally a bronze one slipped in. She turned it and smiled when she heard the click.

She opened the door, stepped quickly inside, and called, "Mom! Dad!" trying to keep the tension out of her voice. She closed the door behind her and waited. The air smelled of lemon oil and rose blossoms. She wasn't sure what she expected to hear, running footsteps, maybe, or the relieved yell of someone who loved her.

Finally she stepped across the tiled entry to the living room. Golden bars of sunshine shot through the windows and reflected off the polished wood floors and heavy, dark furniture. But the room felt too cold. In the overwhelming silence, the ticking of the clock seemed to echo around her.

Comfortable brown-and-gold chairs faced a huge stone fireplace. She turned around, looking for a picture of herself. Anything that would tell her she belonged here. She found nothing.

At last she went back to the hallway and found the stairs that curved up to the second floor. She took the steps two at a time, her backpack banging against her, and almost collided with a wheelchair on the landing. She touched the cold metal handles. It looked too small for an adult. Maybe she had a brother or a sister who had been seriously injured.

Then she glanced down the hallway. Three open doors spilled fading sunlight onto the hall runner. A fourth door at the end was closed. She tiptoed past a long table decorated with crystal vases. The house was deserted, yet she couldn't shake the feeling that someone was there, watching her. She paused and listened before she entered the first room.

Inside the air was thick with disinfectant and medicine smells that seemed incongruous in a room with bright yellow-and-green wallpaper. Games and stuffed animals lay on a hospital bed in the corner. Syringes, pumps, and monitors sat on a long counter next to coloring books and crayons and a tattered game of Monopoly. This room must belong to the brother or sister who used the wheelchair.

She started to step back into the hallway but paused. Something was wrong. The air seemed to be growing colder and her body was filling with a sense of impending danger.

She eased inside the next room. Posters of skateboarders hung on the wall. She smiled. She touched the skates, bats, baseball gloves, knee pads, and helmets lining the shelves. On the desk she spied something that made her heart lurch; doctor's instructions written on Children's Hospital letterhead, and on top of that a long line of brown pill bottles. She picked up the first one and read the name: *Shannon Culbertson*. The last name was different from hers.

Maybe she didn't belong here after all. She glanced at the address on her palm again, the letters and numbers now blurred. The school records said this was her home. Perhaps Shannon was her half sister, or the nurse's records were outdated.

A loud creaking sound made her head jerk around. She waited and listened. Had someone opened a door downstairs? The big house was silent again. She hurried inside the third room and carefully closed the door. This one had to be hers. It definitely belonged to a teenage girl, but she didn't like the decor. The full-size bed was covered with a flowery emerald comforter and lacy pillows, and she felt no sense of familiarity with the white furniture or the pink fabric flowers in the green vase. Was she really the type of girl who would have decorated her room like a flower garden? She didn't think so.

Then she saw the computer. She set her backpack by the nightstand and pressed a button. The computer whined on. Maybe she could find something in the documents stored in the hard drive. She sat down at the desk and stared at the screen, then worked the mouse, but she didn't find any files. There were no e-mails, and it looked as if she had never sent any out. Odd. She shut down the computer, then went to the closet and walked inside. She patted her hand along the wall, searching for a light switch, found it, and turned it on. Her breath caught.

"Wow," she whispered. The clothes definitely looked like something she would wear. Scoop-neck tops and slinky skirts, hipster flare jeans and a leopard camisole. Even the shoes were perfect: Mary Janes with thick, chunky soles, bungee sneakers, and boots. She slipped off her leather jacket, tore off the tag on a fuzzy hooded sweater, and pulled it over her head. She liked the way the sleeves came down to the tips of her fingers. Automatically she poked her thumbs through the weave and smiled.

She stepped back into the bedroom. The tastes in clothes and bedroom decor were too different. She glanced back into the closet, then went to the laundry hamper and lifted the lid. It was empty. She scowled. The clothes looked new and unused. Most still had the sales tags hanging from the side. Even though she couldn't remember her life before this morning, she knew there should be at least one pair of ratty sweats or some dirty clothes.

She started looking through the dresser. In the third drawer, hidden under socks and bras, she found a lined notebook. It looked like a diary. Her hands trembled as she lifted it and opened it to the first page. *Tianna Moore* was written across the top. Her heart began beating rapidly. At last she would have some answers. She had only begun writing in it two days before—the same day she had enrolled in La Brea High. She stretched out on the bed when a sound made her stop. She held her breath and listened.

Stealthy steps quietly crossed the wood floor downstairs. Someone was trying hard to hide their footfalls. That made her alert. A parent or sister wouldn't need to sneak around.

Her hands went cold and she set the diary on the nightstand, careful not to make any sound.

The person was climbing the stairs now. She thought she heard a furtive whisper. She stood and walked silently to the door, paused, and listened, trying to hear what they were saying.

The steps halted on the other side of her bedroom door. A hand brushed against the wood, and then she heard someone squeeze the doorknob. She froze as she watched it slowly turn.

Always trust your instincts. The words came to her suddenly. Who had told her that? No matter. She frantically looked around for a place to hide, then walked back to the bed and slid under it as the door opened.

If the person turned out to be a parent or sibling, she was going to feel very foolish. The comment about paranoid tendencies written on the nurse's computer screen rushed through her mind. Perhaps this was what the notation had meant. Then another thought came to her. Maybe paranoia was sometimes a sane response to what was going on.

She held up the edge of the bedspread with the tips of her fingers and watched as two guys entered the room. They looked about sixteen, not much older than that. The first guy was tall and thin with jagged scars on his bony face. He wore black wire-rim glasses, but the glasses couldn't hide his spooky eyes, which looked piercing enough to penetrate steel. Three silver skull earrings hung from his left ear, and his face was a pincushion: three rings in his nose, two in his lips, and a barbell through his eyebrow.

She felt a shudder of recognition. He was the same guy she had seen in her flashback this afternoon after the ball slammed her face. He looked human enough, but there was also something supernatural about him.

The second guy had the same intensity in his eyes, but he wore a scraggly goatee. A green snake was tattooed on his broad neck, and his dark hair was streaked with orange and yellow. He remained at the door while the bony-faced guy continued into the room.

He stopped near the bed. Her heart lurched. Had he sensed her presence?

Suddenly he leaned over and picked up her backpack.

She banged her head on the thick carpeting, angry at her stupid mistake. How could she have forgotten her backpack?

He lifted the bedspread, and their eyes met with full recognition. She knew him. He wanted to kill her, but she still didn't know why. Her heart beat fiercely.

"Hello, Tianna." He spoke in a sweet, silky voice, as if they had known each other for a long time. His blue eyes sparkled with yellow lights and seemed to bore into her head. His lips curled, but not exactly into a smile—there was too much hate and contempt in it.

"I knew we'd catch you one day, Tianna, I just never expected it to be this easy. You always gave us such fine combat and chase." He seemed truly disappointed.

Instinct told her not to look in his eyes, but it was hard to pull away. Then she realized he had made one big mistake. She smiled, enjoying his sudden confusion. His face was too close to the toe of her boot. She edged her foot back, but something stopped her. Was he controlling her? She didn't think so. It was more a feeling that she couldn't attack, she could only defend. Where had that come from? Some mysterious force inside her seemed to have taken control.

"Come out now." His hand reached for her ankle, and in a flash she made her decision. She knocked his glasses off with the tip of her boot, then kicked again, batting them away. While he was patting the floor, searching for his glasses, she scrambled out the other side of the bed, jumped over it, grabbed her backpack and diary, and ran toward the door.

The guy with the snake tattoo blocked her exit. "Where do you think you're going?"

There was no way she could get around him.

He was enormous, like a football player. She glanced at his face. His eyes held hers, and his thoughts pushed right through her skull. She blinked and shook her head, but she couldn't get rid of the feeling that he was still inside her mind, telling her to go back and sit on the bed.

He laughed at her struggle.

"Sorry," she whispered as she made her decision.

"Sorry?" he repeated.

She brought her leg back as if ready for the goal, but at the last second the mysterious force held her back again and kept her from completing the kick. Instead, she pushed him hard, knocking him off balance. That gave her enough time to dart around him.

He lunged for her like a nose tackle, arms stretched in front of him, and fell flat on his stomach behind her with a loud *oof* as he grabbed her ankle. The table in the hallway skidded and a crystal vase on top rocked back and forth.

"I knew I could count on you to make this fun, Tianna, you always do," the one with the snake   tattoo said as he squeezed her ankle tightly.

"Do I know you?" she asked, trying desperately to kick off her boot.

A startled expression crossed his face. "You don't remember, do you?"

"Remember what?" she yelled back with a surge of adrenaline.

"Justin," he shouted. "She doesn't remember."

"I told you, Mason." Justin's excited voice came from the other room. "You said you hadn't been able to take anything from her, but I knew you got her Tuesday, and you did."

Mason was distracted for an instant, and he loosened his grip. That was all she needed. She yanked back and as she did, her hand accidentally batted the table. The crystal vase tumbled and hit him hard on the top of the head.

"Whoops," she said, even though she knew it couldn't be her fault. She scooted backward, then got up and ran.

He was too large and awkward. She was already at the top of the stairs when he finally stood. At the front door she heard his footsteps thundering behind her. She swung open the door and it hit the wall with a bang. She reached back and closed it, hoping to stall them for precious seconds.

She bounded down the front steps.

A loud crashing sound made her glance back. They had knocked open the door and were following her, eyes glowing.

She tasted fear, her mouth so dry she couldn't swallow, and then she felt their combined mental attack. Against her will she slowed her pace. What kind of creatures were they? She tried to run faster, but her legs begged her to stop. She didn't know how much longer she could fight them. She wanted to surrender and stare into their compelling eyes.

Already she could hear their heavy breathing. They were too close. She was not going to make it.

CHAPTER EIGHT

AT THAT MOMENT Tianna spied a skateboard. Her hand acted on its own, and before she knew what was happening she had grabbed the board, sent it rolling, and jumped on. Two strokes with her right foot, then she pumped, moving her knees from side to side. She curved down the front sidewalk, bumping over the bricks, and just before reaching the front steps, she turned a high ollie and landed on the thick iron banister. She tailslid down the rail, then bent her knees to cushion her landing and kept going.

"Awesome," she breathed, impressed with herself.

She jetted down the middle of the street, the breeze rushing through her hair. She dodged around traffic and eased up on the sidewalk and back out into the street again.

When she was a mile away, she slowed. She didn't know where she was and she didn't care. At least she had gotten away, and apparently she had gone far enough so their powerful mind control couldn't reach her. Why would they want her? There was nothing special about her.

She continued past a parking lot and a taco stand, then looked up and saw that she was at the crossroad of Hollywood Boulevard and Vine. Kids in front of a bar started an impromptu rap. Pedestrians hurried around the hat the kids had set on the sidewalk for tips. She passed a tattoo-and-piercing parlor, a movie memorabilia shop, and a doughnut stand.

Tianna turned the skateboard and wove through tourists gathered around a pink granite star embedded in the sidewalk. She hopped off the curb and sped down the middle of a side street, pumping. She glanced back. No one was following.

When she faced forward again, a black Oldsmobile was racing toward her, engine roaring. She jumped and rode the board over the top of the car, down the back windshield, and off the trunk.

The car screeched to a stop.

She did a one-eighty, whirling around to face the driver and see what kind of damage she had caused, then she did a wheelie stop near the back of the car.

Mason stepped out and grinned at her.

She grabbed the skateboard and heaved it at him, then ran. She ducked behind a line of parked cars and scurried forward, her breath coming in rapid gulps. She scrambled across a parking lot as the sun balanced on the horizon, then crouched low behind a delivery truck. She felt as if she were drowning in her own fear.

She peered from behind the bumper. She couldn't see either of them, but she had an inexplicable feeling that they were close. With a shudder she understood why. An eerie prickling sensation rolled inside her head, and she wondered if they could send out brain waves like some kind of mental radar, searching for her. She knew that she needed to get farther away.

She dodged into an alley that smelled of rotting garbage and kicked through newspapers and broken beer bottles, then climbed a Cyclone fence. The gate swayed back and forth like a snake trying to shake her off. She jumped from the top and landed in the trash that had swept against the bottom of the wire mesh.

She sprinted past a rusted Dumpster and stopped, then twirled around, the stench unbearable. She had boxed herself in. She heard a sound and turned. Justin had the toe of his shoe in the wire mesh and started to climb the fence.

"Hi, Tianna." Mason stood beside him, casting a huge shadow down the alley.

CHAPTER NINE

JUSTIN GRINNED AT HER as his hand reached the top of the gate. She let out a sigh. This was it. She wished the mesh in the fence were too small for his feet.

Abruptly he slipped. He slid down the front of the fence and landed on the ground. He looked back at her, surprised, then over at Mason. "I thought you said you got her."

"I did," Mason explained.

"Well, then, did she get her memories back?" Justin asked.

Mason cautioned him to be quiet. "Shut

up!" He scowled and looked back at Tianna.

Justin tried again to push the toe of his shoe into the mesh, but this time it didn't fit. "We still have you," he shouted angrily.

"She has to come out this way," Mason agreed, and motioned to Justin. They walked back to the entrance of the alley.

"We'll be waiting for you, Tianna," Justin said, taunting her.

She knew he was right. That was the only way to get out, and already she could feel their thoughts piercing through her mind, telling her to surrender.

She took refuge behind the Dumpster. Those guys weren't ordinary people, but then she smiled to herself. She was beginning to think that she was no ordinary girl. For the second time today, she had thought something and it had happened. She hated to think that she had actually broken Michelle's ankle. That had never been her intent, but she had desperately wanted the mesh to become smaller, and it had. Could it have just been a coincidence? She hoped not.

She leaned against a brick wall and studied a stack of old newspapers next to a crate of blackened lettuce leaves. In her mind's eye she pictured the edges moving.

She watched in wonder as the stale newsprint fluttered.

She sucked in her breath. Had it only been her imagination? Now she let her mind expand. She pictured the pages opening, and they did.

"Cool," she whispered, and smiled. "Now dance around the alley."

The papers wavered, then glided about in a strange collage, flapping like the wings of giant cranes.

She turned away, and the papers fell to the ground again. She saw an apple core. She imagined it flying over the fence and landing at Justin's feet.

The apple core zipped away. She peeked from behind the Dumpster as it landed in front of Justin.

He picked up the apple core and turned. In the instant their eyes met, he knew.

"Good luck catching me now!" she yelled at him.

He nudged Mason and they both started walking down the alley toward the fence. The air shimmered in front of them with purple heat waves seeping from their eyes.

"Too late," she said. "You had your chance." She darted behind the Dumpster. She had heard about telekinetic phenomena. Where she had heard about it she didn't know, but she knew telekinesis was the ability to move objects by thinking about them. She felt thrilled with the possibilities of her newfound power.

She wondered if she could move larger things, too. She glanced at the Dumpster, narrowed her eyes in concentration, and strained. The side of the Dumpster buckled with a sharp pop. She gasped. Could she bend objects, too?

A noise like rattling chains startled her, and she peered back down the alley. Justin and Mason were shaking the double gate in the fence as if they were trying to break the chain lock. She turned back to the trash piled at the dead end and raised her hands like a great conductor of an orchestra. Soon lettuce leaves, orange peels, coffee grounds, and papers were flying everywhere. With a flick of her wrists, the garbage bounced away from her, heading for Justin and Mason.

Without warning she let everything fall. Trash and garbage rained down on them. She laughed, and even though she could feel the sting of their minds, she didn't turn away yet.

Windows above her opened and people leaned over their sills, staring down into the alley.

"What's going on?" a woman screamed.

Tianna looked up. That's when she saw the fire escape over her head.

When the woman ducked back inside her apartment, Tianna concentrated and willed the iron ladder to lower. It did. She picked up her backpack, swung it over her shoulders, grabbed the rung, and climbed up to the fire escape. She continued up the stairs until she found an open window.

Cautiously she climbed inside a stranger's apartment and tiptoed toward what she thought must be the front door. She had her hand on the doorknob, twisting it, when a young woman came out from another room, carrying a baby in her arms. She stopped and stared, speechless, at Tianna.

"Oops, wrong apartment." Tianna hurried out the door, then continued down the long hallway to the fire stairs and outside.

She walked in the cool evening air and took a deep breath, feeling safe at last. She had started to pass a storefront when someone grabbed her arm and yanked her inside.

CHAPTER TEN

TIANNA TURNED, READY to defend herself. "Jimena," she sighed, and let her hands drop back to her sides.

"*Estás escamada,*" Jimena whispered, and her eyes darted outside as if she were searching for the danger. "What scared you?"

Tianna shook her head. "I'm not afraid."

"*Mentirosa.* Why do you always lie to me? Your fingers are cold and trembling. What happened?" Jimena gazed at her with her witching eyes, all dark and smoldering as if she were working some kind of black magic on her, then the moment ended and Jimena shook her head and scowled. "What's with you? Don't you know how dangerous it is out there? What were you doing walking down those streets alone, anyway?"

Tianna searched for an excuse, then drew back. What made Jimena think it was any of her business? "I was just taking in the sights like any tourist," she lied defiantly.

"Well, don't," Jimena warned her. "Not in this part of town. You don't understand how *peligroso* it is at night here."

"Are you talking about gangbangers or drug users?" Tianna snickered. "I'm not scared of them." She wondered what Jimena would do if she knew what kind of strange creatures had been chasing her.

"You think I'm talking about some *vato loco* or a *tecato*. You don't even know."

Jimena's dismissive manner angered Tianna. She started to say something and stopped. She couldn't tell Jimena what had really happened, and even if she did, there was no way Jimena would believe her.

"Maybe you'd better rest here for a while." Jimena softened suddenly.

"Do I look like I need to rest?" Tianna glared at her.

"After the way you played soccer today, you deserve a rest." Jimena smiled, her charm rekindled, and once again there was something captivating about the way her eyes sparkled. "You were awesome. Come on. You can't go back out there now. I'll give you a ride home after."

"After what?" Tianna asked.

Jimena lifted a heavy black curtain and Tianna looked inside, surprised. She had thought the storefront was vacant, but she was in some kind of performance bar.

Kids were crowded around a foot-high stage. Serena stood there under the only light in the entire room, reciting poetry. She looked beautiful, all in black, her eyes sad and cast down, reading from a sheet of paper, her lips against a mike.

Tianna nudged through the crowd behind Jimena, then squeezed into a seat at a table and shoved her backpack underneath. Graffiti with disturbing messages covered the tabletop.

A girl with multiple piercings and red eye shadow around bleary eyes set a bowl of gummy bears on the table and handed Tianna a menu.

"Go ahead and order." Jimena sipped an oversized latte. "I'll treat."

"I've got money," Tianna lied. She didn't really have any that she could spare. She needed every dime to run away.

"Yeah, but you need your *plata*." Jimena looked at her knowingly. "I can recognize someone who's on the run."

She started to protest but stopped. "Thanks. I'll have a mocha."

"De nada." Jimena smiled.

Minutes later the waitress brought back a cup the size of a soup bowl filled with steaming chocolate-flavored coffee and topped with whipped cream and chocolate shavings. Tianna realized she hadn't eaten anything since the bite of muffin early in the morning.

She sipped the brew, enjoying the rich, sweet taste, and listened to Serena recite a poem about her demon lover. It made Tianna think more than ever that Serena was some kind of witch or worse. How could she know so much about temptation and choosing between good and evil? The words sent chills through Tianna. She glanced around the room. Celebrities in sweats and baseball caps trying to be inconspicuous sat next to punks, goths, gangbangers, and students from UCLA. All of them seemed captivated by Serena's words.

Tianna liked the artsy vibration. Canvases of new art hung next to poems kids had written on the walls in large letters with Day-Glo felt markers.

Serena started another poem about the moon and hope.

"She's good, huh?" Jimena whispered.

Tianna started to say yes, but a guy with a safety pin through his eyebrow shot them a warning look, and instead she only nodded and glanced back at the stage.

Finally Serena finished and walked back toward Tianna and Jimena. Kids were shaking her hand and asking for copies of her poetry.

Jimena stood. "Come on, we'll meet her out front."

When they got to the door, Jimena opened it and looked cautiously up and down the street.

"Who are you looking for?" Tianna asked, wondering what Jimena had expected to see.

"Just being careful." Jimena smiled. "My car's parked a block away."

They started walking, and soon Serena caught up to them.

"Great game," she congratulated Tianna.

"Thanks. I loved your poetry." Tianna returned the compliment, then she looked at Jimena. She had forgotten to ask. "Did we win?"

"Decca never got a goal past Jimena," Serena announced proudly. "She was incredible."

"Yeah, but we needed the goal Tianna made," Jimena added, and then her mood became more serious. "What did you see out here tonight that frightened you, Tianna?"

"Nothing." Tianna wasn't in the mood to answer questions. Maybe she should go to the bus station. "Look, I live close by," she lied. "I think I'll just walk."

"It's safer if you stay with us," Jimena said as they passed a Laundromat with its smells of bleach and detergent drifting into the air.

"Why?" Tianna asked, wondering what they knew. "What's so dangerous in this area of town?"

"Just your normal freaks and perverts," Serena answered with a grin. "They like to hang out here."

Tianna glanced at her to see if she was teasing. She looked dead serious, but Tianna had a feeling that there was more she wasn't saying, and then her eyes changed. It was startling the way her pupils opened and dilated. At the same time Tianna felt a black wave rush across her mind, followed by a tingling, as if worms were crawling through her brain. Had Serena done that? Or were Justin and Mason back? She studied the old storefront buildings behind her, lit up by blue, green, and pink neon lights. Nothing looked menacing, and the odd feeling in her head was gone now, anyway. Maybe she was only supertired and hungry.

"Was someone chasing you?" Serena asked unexpectedly.

Tianna looked back at her. "Why would you ask that?"

"Just if you were afraid, I thought maybe someone had been bothering you." Serena glanced behind them as if she were checking the street for danger.

At the same time Jimena seemed to study the shadows in an odd way.

"What are you looking for?" Tianna asked nervously.

Serena grabbed her arm. She had that same enchantress smile as Jimena. "You know, don't you? Do you want to talk about it?"

Tianna stopped. What did Serena mean? She felt a rush of confusion, and then anger took over. "I just wish you'd both go away and stop bothering me."

They looked at her, surprised.

And in an instant she realized she had made a wish. "I don't mean it," she added quickly, terrified that her thought might make something happen to them. She hated to think she could actually make people disappear, but she didn't understand her power yet and she didn't want to harm them accidentally the way she had hurt Michelle.

Jimena and Serena looked at her oddly, and under the streetlight a gold aura seemed to flutter around them and billow out into the cold night. Then suddenly Jimena stared at her, sightless, as if she were in a trance.

Tianna felt the blood rush from her head, and she had to grab the fender of a parked Toyota to keep from swaying. What had she done this time? Jimena looked bad. She glanced at Serena. She still seemed normal. At least she hadn't harmed them both.

"I'm so sorry," Tianna whispered. "I didn't mean to hurt her. I just didn't want you to ask me any more questions."

"Hurt who?" Serena stepped closer, her eyes compassionate.

"Jimena," Tianna blurted. "Look at her. I didn't want to do that."

Serena turned slowly and looked at Jimena. She acted as if she were used to seeing Jimena stare sightless into the night.

"What do you mean?" Serena asked.

"I put Jimena in some kind of stupor," Tianna confessed with growing panic. "Can't you see? She's not moving. Maybe we should get her to the hospital."

Serena snickered. "She's fine." But then she turned back with a swiftness that made Tianna flinch. "But why would you think you had done that to her?"

Tianna leaned over the back of the car, trying to gather her thoughts. The metal felt cold and comforting against her flushed cheek. "I did it. You don't understand what I can do."

Serena patted Tianna's back as if she were trying to comfort her. "Why don't you tell me what you're talking about."

"I broke Michelle's ankle," Tianna confessed.

"You couldn't have," Serena answered. "I was watching the whole time. You were too far away."

Tianna pushed herself up, ready to explain everything, but before she could, Jimena shuddered and a smile crossed her face. She glanced at Tianna, then Serena, as if nothing strange had just transpired.

"Did you see something?" Serena asked Jimena in a low voice.

Jimena nodded. Happiness seemed to bubble inside her and spill over into the night air.

"I can't wait to hear." Serena's eagerness matched Jimena's.

Tianna felt relieved. She hadn't done anything to Jimena. But then she felt flustered. If she hadn't put Jimena in a trance, what had just happened? Quickly, new apprehension took hold. Jimena must have been working a spell, trying to divine something, and Serena had known all along what she was doing. Apparently the spell had worked. Jimena had seen something, but what? Tianna had a creepy feeling it involved her.

"Okay, here's the car." Jimena pulled out a key on a silver chain and stepped to an '81 Oldsmobile that sparkled as if it were new.

"Nice car," Tianna said.

"It belongs to my brother," Jimena explained. "He lets me drive it when he's home from San Diego even though I don't have a license yet."

"You don't?" Tianna wondered if it was safe to ride with her.

Jimena smiled and seemed to read her thoughts. "I'm safe. I learned how to drive jacking cars."

"So it's true what I heard about you?" Tianna stared at her in disbelief.

"It's not like she does it anymore," Serena put in, and then she changed the subject. "Tianna was worried she did something to you, Jimena."

Jimena glanced at Tianna, her eyes laughing. "Why would you think that?"

"You looked odd," Tianna answered. "That's all." She really didn't want to say any more. She wanted to get away from them.

"I'm sorry you were worried. I'm fine," Jimena reassured her.

"She thinks she broke Michelle's ankle." Serena opened the car door.

"I wished it," Tianna mumbled. "But I didn't really want it to happen."

Then they both laughed.

"You're so superstitious," Serena said. "Is that all?"

"Yeah, a wish can't make something come true," Jimena added. "If it could, half the people walking around would be dead."

Tianna didn't say more. Let them think whatever they wanted. She was never going to see them again after this night, anyway.

If she'd had any doubt before, she was convinced now that Jimena and Serena were witches. She wondered if the guys chasing her could be some kind of warlocks who belonged to the same clan. She didn't think so. Jimena and Serena seemed too nice, and Justin and Mason had an aura of evil about them.

"Get in," Jimena said. "I'll give you a ride home."

"Come on," Serena coaxed. "It's safer with us than on the street."

Tianna looked back at the night. She wanted

to go to the bus station and leave now, but it might take her hours to find it. Besides, she felt too tired to walk, and she definitely didn't want to run into Justin and Mason again. Reluctantly she opened the car door and slid inside.

Jimena turned the ignition. Music boomed from the speakers, making Tianna's heart vibrate with the beat.

CHAPTER ELEVEN

"**D**ON'T YOU REMEMBER where you live?" Jimena asked after traveling down Wilshire Boulevard between the La Brea Tar Pits and Ralph's grocery store for the fourth time.

"It's nearby," Tianna answered. She could picture the apartment clearly in her mind. She just didn't know where to find it. "Someplace around here. I just moved in."

Serena glanced at her watch again. "It's getting late. I promised my dad I'd be home before eight."

"I think if you just turn right at the next

block." Tianna wished she hadn't taken the ride with them. Why had she assumed she would be able to remember enough to find her way back to the apartment building? Los Angeles was huge.

"Serena, would you find out?" Jimena asked impatiently, and shut off the music.

The silence made Tianna's ears ring.

"How's she going to know?" Tianna started to ask, but stopped suddenly.

Serena leaned over the car seat. There was something uncanny about the way her eyes dilated, as if some kind of power were building inside her. Tianna wanted to look away, but she felt compelled to stare. It wasn't frightening, but warm and soothing in a dreamy way, even though she didn't like the inexplicable feeling of fingers wiggling through her brain.

Then suddenly the feeling was gone and Serena looked at her with fascination. "It's one of the old apartment buildings over by Ralph's on Wilshire," she said to Jimena. "We've passed the street already."

Tianna braced herself as Jimena made a big

looping U-turn and started down Wilshire in the opposite direction.

"How did you know?" Tianna asked, amazed. "You saw . . . did you read my mind? You did."

Serena laughed, and the sound was magical. "No one can do that."

"But you did," Tianna said, dismayed. "I felt something when you looked at me."

"You couldn't have," Serena insisted. "Because I didn't."

"Then how did you know where I live?" Tianna didn't believe her. She wondered what else she might have seen. Did she know she couldn't remember anything before this morning? Or that she planned to run away?

"That one." Serena pointed.

Jimena pulled the car over to the side of the road in front of the same apartment building that Tianna had left earlier that day. She pressed the brake hard and turned off the car engine.

"Thanks." Tianna grabbed her backpack and hurried to get out. She had had enough of these two. They were nice, but way spooky. Before she could open the door, Serena turned back and locked it. She kept her finger on the lock, pressing down.

"Now we need some answers, Tianna." Serena spoke softly. "What are you running from?"

"That's a strange thing to ask," Tianna answered.

"If you knew everything about us, you wouldn't think it was," Serena explained. "Jimena and I can help you. Do you know why they want you?"

"No one's chasing me," Tianna insisted.

"I'm pretty sure I know who is after you," Serena said. "But I don't understand why."

"Couldn't you see?" Jimena asked, looking baffled.

"There was nothing to see," Serena explained to Jimena.

"How can that be?" Jimena jerked around and stared at Tianna in amazement.

Serena shrugged. "Everything was blank. She only has a few memories."

"You did read my mind." Tianna accused her angrily.

Serena smiled sheepishly. "Only because we want to help you."

Tianna used the moment to bat Serena's hand away, unlock the car, and scramble outside.

"Hey!" Serena called after her. "Come back."

"No way!" Tianna yelled.

Jimena opened the car door and shouted after her, "You need our help, Tianna."

"I don't want you to help me."

Their offer to help only made her uneasy. How could she trust them after the strange way they had behaved? Besides, all she wanted to do was eat, sleep, and run. Tomorrow at dawn she was going to be on a Greyhound, waving goodbye to L.A. and all its crazy people.

Tianna rushed into the apartment building and slammed the door, half afraid Serena and Jimena would chase after her. She glanced out the side window and watched Jimena's car pull away from the curb. She let out a sigh. She was starving and hoped there was something good in the refrigerator.

Her excitement was building as she ran up the stairs. Maybe there would be someone waiting for her inside with a big cheese pizza, chocolate-chip cookies, and a huge glass of milk. And if someone were there, then she wouldn't have to run away. She would have a home and someone who loved and cared for her.

As she reached the landing, Hanna stepped in front of her.

"There you are." Hanna popped a green olive in her mouth. "I've been waiting for you." The smells coming from inside Hanna's apartment made Tianna's stomach grumble. She breathed deeply, inhaling in the warm spicy smells.

"Why?" Tianna asked impatiently. Her stomach felt as if it had acid in it.

"I have a favor to ask." Hanna smiled.

"Sure," Tianna said. "Right after dinner. I'll come back."

"It's really quite urgent," Hanna insisted. "My friends and I need a fourth person for our séance."

"Séance?" Tianna couldn't believe what she was hearing. This day wouldn't get any weirder.

"Won't you join us?" Hanna pleaded. "We have to have a fourth person to make our circle complete."

Tianna shook her head. "Sorry." That was the last thing in the world she wanted to do. With everything else that had happened today, she didn't need to see a ghost, too. "No, but thanks for asking."

She started to dart away, but Hanna grabbed her hand.

"I made my beef brisket," Hanna coaxed. "Everyone says it's delicious. After dinner we'll pull out the Ouija board. The séance won't take longer than an hour. You'll still have time to study."

"Another night. I think my mom's waiting for me," Tianna said, eager to get away.

"If you change your mind," Hanna yelled after her, "there's still time. We won't start until after we eat."

"Okay," Tianna called over her shoulder.

The door to her apartment was unlocked. She didn't remember locking it when she ran out that morning. She entered and quickly closed it behind her. The interior still smelled of Pine-Sol and looked the same as when she had left it earlier. She tossed her backpack on the bed and opened the refrigerator. It was empty except for a box of baking soda. She quickly looked through cupboards and drawers. All were barren.

The truth hit her, and she sat on the bed with a heavy sigh. She was a squatter. She didn't somehow rent the apartment. This had never been her home. She had broken into it.

Now the aromas of onions and coffee coming from Hanna's apartment were more than she could bear.

CHAPTER TWELVE

HANNA'S APARTMENT WAS larger than the one Tianna had claimed. There was a small kitchen off the living room and a bedroom in the back down a long hallway. Tianna sat at a round dining table, eating off sparkling white china. A small oscillating fan on the sideboard swung lazily back and forth, making the edge of the red tablecloth float up, then down.

"That's the best brisket I've ever made, if I do say so myself," Hanna announced.

Tianna nodded and scooped more gravy onto her potatoes. "You're a great cook," she repeated for perhaps the fourth time. "Everything's delicious."

"It doesn't look like you're going to have any problem with leftovers." Hanna's friend Sylvia smirked. She had red hair like a flame and wore a long gray dress with three strings of pearls.

"I used to eat like that when I was young," Hanna's sister, Trudy, put in. She was a short chubby woman with a walker.

Tianna glanced up. They were watching her. Then she realized she was the only one still eating.

"Do you want some more peas, dear?" Hanna asked, and handed her the bowl.

"No, thanks." Tianna put down her fork.

Hanna slapped the sides of the table, making the silverware jingle. "Let's get this cleared and into the dishwasher, then we can start."

Tianna stood. Her stomach felt stuffed, but the feeling was a good one.

After the table was cleared and the dishes neatly stacked in the dishwasher, Hanna placed candles about the room, then arranged more in a circle in the middle of the table around a Ouija board.

"So who are you trying to contact?" Tianna pushed her hair back.

Hanna turned and smiled at her, eyes misting. "Skinanbone."

"Skinanbone?" Tianna asked.

"My Chihuahua, may he rest in peace." Hanna reverentially placed a tiny black dog collar with silver studs on the table near the Ouija board. A small gold heart and dog license tags were attached to a metal clasp near the buckle.

Then Hanna and Sylvia each took a book of matches and started lighting the candles. Wicks sparked and wisps of smoke made serpentine patterns in the air. The flames bent sideways each time they caught the breeze from the fan.

Trudy sadly pointed to a picture on the piano of a Chihuahua wearing a red sweater. "That's Skinanbone."

"What happened to him?" Tianna asked as Hanna turned off the lights.

Sylvia pulled out her chair and sat down.

"Another dog just grabbed him up and stole him away."

"That's horrible," Tianna said.

Trudy pointed to a corner of the room and whispered, "Hanna still hasn't been able to clear out his things."

A red pillow sat next to a comfortable chair. Dog toys were piled high in a basket.

"That's where Skinanbone slept while I watched TV," Hanna added as she joined them.

Sylvia nodded. "They always watched the nightly news together. They both loved weather."

"Shall we hold hands and begin?" Hanna had a solemn look. "We do the séance first," she explained to Tianna, "and try to call up his spirit. Then we use the Ouija board and see if he has anything to communicate."

Tianna nodded and Hanna clasped her hand tightly, then Sylvia grasped her other hand and their circle was complete.

There was a moment of silence. Tianna wasn't sure what to do.

Hanna looked up, took a deep breath, then

closed her eyes and whistled, loud and long. "Here, Skinanbone," she called. "Here, boy, come home to Mommy."

Tianna bit her lower lip and glanced around the table. Sylvia's eyes were closed and her head was back, lifted toward the ceiling in total concentration, and Trudy gazed upward with a hopeful expression.

"Say something, Trudy," Hanna urged. "He was always close to you."

"Come here, Skinanbone." Trudy spoke dramatically. "Your mommy's been crying for you."

Tianna could sense how much the women missed Skinanbone. Maybe she could make them feel as if they had contacted him. It would be her thank-you for such a tasty and generous dinner. That was the least she could do.

She concentrated on the dog collar until it lifted into the air to where she imagined Skinanbone's neck might be if he were standing on the table. Then she jiggled it from side to side as though the dog were shaking his head.

Hanna's eyes burst open. "Skinanbone!"

"Is it really him?" Sylvia asked, and opened her eyes. "Oh, my."

"What?" Trudy looked from one woman to the other.

"Look," Hanna shouted.

Tianna wiggled the dog collar again.

"He's back," Trudy declared. "Praise be."

"We miss you, you sweet little puppy," Hanna said in a babyish voice. "How is doggie heaven?"

Tianna concentrated again. This was harder to do, but finally she made the dog collar fly from the table in a natural arc as if Skinanbone had leapt from it. Then she moved the collar over to the doggie bed in the corner and used her power to press into the red pillow below the collar to make it look as if tiny paws were walking over it.

"Hanna, look!" Trudy motioned with her head.

"What?" Hanna asked.

"His box!" Sylvia shouted. "Look at his box!"

Tianna focused, trying to make the tiny paw

prints circle the way dogs do before they settle for a nap.

"He always made me dizzy when he did that," Trudy said in a wistful voice, then she sighed. "He was such a sweetie."

Tianna slipped deeper and deeper into herself as she concentrated more. She made the collar rush to the box of dog toys, then tried to make it appear as if a very small dog ghost had bitten into a ball and was dashing away with it.

The women squealed.

"He wants to play," Hanna exclaimed happily.

Suddenly the voices of the women became fainter, then Tianna's vision blurred and the room seemed to shift as though she were hovering over it and far away. Reality wrinkled, and it was as if Tianna were looking at everything through pebbled glass.

She blinked and shook her head, but that didn't make things move back the way they had been before. She could no longer hear Hanna, Sylvia, or Trudy. There was only a rushing sound like wind or water.

At last the glass rippled and broke apart, and she was alone in a cold and murky place. It was like being in the middle of nowhere, but something about it was familiar, as if she had seen it before. She felt on the verge of recalling some important memory.

Then the air around her stirred and a white cloud formed from churning mists and came toward her. A girl about her age floated in the delicate vapor. She sensed something good about her and thought perhaps she was some kind of guardian angel, one that had no wings.

The girl looked at Tianna with frightened eyes, but the fear only made her beauty more divine. Tianna wondered if she had known her once in this life before something tragic had happened and she had passed on to the other side.

"Go," the girl mouthed, and waved her hands as if warning Tianna away.

She looked behind her. Where could she go? Nothingness surrounded her. She wondered if she had broken into heaven, but then behind the girl a black-night shadow formed. Crimson waves shimmered from the dark form, and Tianna knew it was more likely she had fallen into hell. There was something unholy about the dusky shape, and the cold emanating from it. She began to shiver.

The black vapor twirled, then swept toward her. The girl tried to stop it, but the demon shadow twisted around her and shot at Tianna with a speed that made the air vibrate.

Tianna shrieked and screamed again, knowing it had her.

Then she felt warm hands touching her cheeks. She shook her head, and suddenly she was back in Hanna's living room and everyone was staring at her.

Sylvia held her arm and Hanna patted her face.

"Don't be scared," Hanna said, "Skinanbone was a loving little pup." There were tears in her eyes. "He would never, ever hurt you. I promise, dear."

"You'd love him if you ever met him in real life," Trudy added.

But Sylvia continued to stare at her oddly.

"Tianna has some kind of special power," Sylvia remarked.

"What do you mean?" Tianna asked in a shaky voice.

"We've never been able to make contact with Skinanbone before," Sylvia said. "But tonight we could because you're here."

"And what happened, dear?" Hanna asked. "You were in a trance or something. We had a hard time waking you."

"Mediums always do that," Trudy said. "You know that, Hanna. They have to go into a trance to call up the dead."

Tianna's heart beat rapidly, and she wondered if she had actually made contact with the spirit world. She glanced about her. The shadows in the living room all had a bloodred cast now and a strange texture as if they were solid and warm.

She knocked back her chair and rushed from the room.

CHAPTER THIRTEEN

TIANNA CAUTIOUSLY ENTERED her apartment and looked around. A sudden scraping sound startled her. She glanced at the window and thought she saw a face staring back at her, but quickly realized it was only the limb of a tree. The twiggy branches continued to grate across the glass. She shut the door and flicked on the light. Everything seemed normal, but she couldn't stop the shaking of her hands.

Footsteps in the hallway made her alert. She listened carefully to the voices, but the people didn't sound as if they were trying not to be heard.

She pressed her ear against the wood anyway. They walked right by. Fear was clouding her thinking and making her too edgy. She tried to convince herself that she would be secure here for the night. At least she hoped she would be, but she wondered if she could ever feel safe anywhere again.

"What am I going to do?" she said aloud, trying to give herself comfort, but the tremor in her voice only made her more afraid.

She considered what had happened in Hanna's apartment. It felt as if she had lifted some kind of barrier and uncovered another world. She shuddered. The shadow had felt completely evil.

Slowly she took off her boots and wiggled her toes. Maybe that other world was the dimension she belonged in. Could it be that Mason and Justin were only trying to take her home? She shook her head. She didn't think so.

The bed looked inviting. She needed to lie down and sleep. She felt exhausted, but she was afraid to stay in this tiny, enclosed space. It could too easily become a trap. She stared at the dark shape of the hulking tree pressing against the window. Maybe that was a possibility. She opened the window. The screen was already gone. She looked down. It rested in the lawn under the bluish light of a security lamp. She must have crawled in through this window the night before. She leaned out now and looked up.

It felt safer to sleep on the roof, and she thought she could use the tree to crawl up there. Within minutes she had rolled a pink blanket and the bedspread into a tight ball, then tied them to her backpack, swung both onto her back, crawled out the window onto the branch, and used the tree limbs to climb to the roof.

Her body began to unwind. It felt safer here under the stars. She curled into her blanket and rested her head on her backpack, gazing up at the moon. She noticed that it was on its waning cycle and almost dark. Her heart started beating rapidly. She didn't understand why the ebbing moon should fill her with such a growing sense of urgency, but it did. She felt that there was something important she was supposed to do, but she couldn't remember what.

CHAPTER FOURTEEN

TIANNA WOKE WITH the gentle feeling of sunshine warming her face and an opulent deep turquoise sky over her head. She stretched and smiled, recalling yesterday. As horrible as the day had been, it was still a sweet pleasure to be able to have some memory of her life before this moment.

The aromas of biscuits and coffee drifted up to her, and she wondered idly what Hanna was fixing for breakfast. She thought about last night. Now, in the daylight with a soft breeze caressing her face, what had happened in Hanna's apartment seemed unreal. She tried to recall how dead scared she had felt, but the feeling of terror had slipped away in her slumber. Maybe she had fallen asleep at the table after all and only conjured the girl in her dream. She had been in a torpor from such a big meal. She had probably dozed off. Maybe she should try again and see.

She rolled up her blanket, grabbed her backpack, and crawled down the tree. Everything inside the small apartment looked the same. She shut the window behind her and threw her bundle and backpack on the bed. She wanted something to eat, but first on her list was a long, hot shower. She stepped into the small bathroom, turned the spigot, stripped, and climbed under the luxurious spray.

It felt too dangerous to stay in Los Angeles, and fortunately she had enough money to buy a bus ticket, so as soon as she dressed, she was going to leave. She didn't know why Justin and Mason wanted her so badly, but she didn't need to stick around and discover the reason.

She turned off the water and stepped out.

There were no towels in the bathroom, so she pulled the sheet from the bed and wrapped it tightly around her. She sat in the sunshine cascading into the room and worked a comb through her hair. She thought again about the strange sensation yesterday of going into another dimension. She was more curious than afraid now and wondered if she could make it happen again.

Maybe it was part of her power. She tried to ignore the compulsion to return to that other world and focused instead on untangling her long black hair. It could be risky. Last night Hanna had been there and she had pulled her back somehow, but now she was alone. What would happen if she couldn't get back to reality?

She flipped the comb aside. Why was she hesitating? It wasn't like she had anything to lose. She couldn't recall her family or her friends, and just possibly what had happened to her had something to do with that other place. More than anything she wanted to remember so she could get back home. It was worth a try. Besides, how was she going to learn how to leave that realm unless she went there and came back? She'd only stay for a moment. It had probably been a dream, anyway, so why wait? Find out now.

She stared at the wall. The wind sighed and brushed through the tree branches outside and made spangled sunlight sway back and forth across the apartment in a mesmerizing way. She concentrated and tried to use the same mental energy she had used last night to put the paw prints in Skinanbone's pillow.

Soon the gray-green paint bubbled. Then the plaster buckled and crumbled away, exposing the laths. The thin boards snapped and a swirl of dust climbed into the air. At last her vision blurred and the world seemed far away, as if she were looking through gritty textured glass. It wavered, then shattered, and Tianna was no longer in the small apartment but back in that other place.

Almost immediately she saw the same girl floating toward her. She didn't look as frightened as she had the night before, but something still seemed wrong with her.

"How did you get here?" the girl whispered, and looked behind her as if she were scared the shadow cloud might appear again. She seemed weakened and languishing, as if this dreary place was stealing her strength.

"Are you all right?" Tianna asked.

"You shouldn't be here," the girl warned her, and Tianna had the impression that something bad was happening to her. Her eyes, so bright the night before, looked joyless now.

"Where am I?" Tianna looked at the gloomy mists roiling around the girl. Were they sucking energy from her?

The girl started to answer, but then the fear crept back in her eyes. "Leave!"

"I'm not sure I know how," Tianna answered, and realized she had made a foolish mistake. She had never really believed she'd be able to get back here, and now that she was, she didn't know how to go.

"You can't stay," the girl insisted.

"Why not?" Tianna glanced nervously around her, but she didn't see anything to suggest danger, and she wanted to find out if the girl knew anything about her past. Maybe she held the key that could unlock Tianna's memories.

The girl seemed panicked now. "Don't you feel it? It knows you're here and it's coming for you."

"What knows I'm here?" Tianna asked, and at the same moment Tianna felt her body collapse under a heavy weight that filled the air with a pernicious chill.

"Leave!" the girl repeated harshly.

"How?" Tianna rubbed her arms against the cold.

The girl shrugged. "If I knew, I wouldn't be here."

"How did you get here?" Tianna asked, and reached for her hand. "Maybe we can escape together."

The girl jerked her hand back. "It's too late for me. Just save yourself."

The air closed in tightly and Tianna started to tremble as dread spread through her. She didn't see anything, but then she heard a loud whoosh and the shadow funneled into the murk-iness.

The dark form hovered briefly, undulating as it grew. Tianna felt awestruck, unable to pull her eyes away. The strange cloud was beautiful in its own evil way, like a fierce approaching storm. Then suddenly it soared at her as if it had a will and a vicious human intent to destroy her.

"Run!" the girl urged. "Go. Don't let it catch you."

"Where?" Tianna looked around her. Every-where appeared exactly the same. It was like being in the middle of the ocean without a sun. She dashed away, wanting to scream, but her mouth felt too dry.

The sheet she had wrapped around her ham-pered her speed. She had only gotten a little way when hands reached from the shadows and held her tight.

"No!" she screamed, struggling against the warm arms circling her.

Suddenly, it was as if a veil had ripped

between the two worlds and she was back in reality. Sunlight glared in her face.

She glanced around, still filled with panic, and was surprised to see that she now stood in front of the apartment building. When she had run from the menacing cloud in that other realm, she must have somehow changed location in this world as well. She was about to start back to the apartment when she realized someone's arms were still wrapped tightly around her. Her head whipped back to see who held her.

"Derek!" she shouted, and realized suddenly that she only had the sheet covering her.

"You were out here running like crazy," he explained, and released his hold. "You didn't hear me when I called your name. I figured something was wrong, so I caught you. What were you running from?"

She felt grateful and embarrassed at the same time. He had pulled her back and saved her from the shadow. She tightened her hold on the sheet, and Derek didn't bother to take his eyes away.

"I thought I heard a woman scream that

someone had taken her purse," she lied. "So I came outside to help."

"Like that?" He smirked.

"I sleep in the nude." It was the first thing that came to mind and it was also the worst thing to say. She rolled her eyes at his silly grin. "Look, in an emergency you don't have time to put on clothes."

He snickered. "Get dressed. I'll give you a ride to school." He pointed to a blue Ford Escort parked at the curb.

They started walking back to the apartment building. Her knees still felt shaky and twice she cast glances behind her just to make sure the shadow hadn't left its world and followed her here. She wondered what it was.

Then she stopped suddenly and eyed Derek suspiciously. "How did you know where I live?"

"I asked Michael," he explained.

"Michael knew?" She felt surprised and elated at the same time.

"Not at first," Derek said. "Michael asked Vanessa and Vanessa asked Jimena."

"Michael did all that to find out where I live?"

"For me," Derek added as they started up the steps.

"For you?" She stopped at the door and looked at him.

He blushed and didn't answer her.

"Wait here, Derek." She went inside and left him on the porch. "I'll just run upstairs and change and I'll be right back down."

"If you hurry, we can stop at Starbucks for a muffin and coffee," he offered.

"I'll hurry." But she had no intention of coming back. She was going to dress, then climb out using the tree and head for the bus stop. By the time Derek realized she was gone, she would be drinking coffee on a Greyhound.

She ran up the stairs, the sheet tangling behind her, and passed Hanna, leaving for work, the same two shopping bags clasped in her hands.

"Morning," she said, then she tried her door. It was locked.

She heard Hanna's kind laughter and turned.

"You have to be more careful," Hanna explained. "It's too easy to lock yourself out of these apartments. And look at you! What were you trying to figure out? How to fix a sheet for a toga party or something?"

Tianna nodded, but she had no idea what a toga party was.

"I didn't even think they had them anymore."

"Mom already left," Tianna said. "Can you help me?"

"I've got an extra key," Hanna explained, and started to unlock her apartment door. "The last tenant asked me to hold on to it for emergencies just like this. It might still work. I'll be right back."

Tianna waited patiently as Hanna disappeared into her apartment. When she came back to the hallway, she pinched a brass key in her fingers.

"I wanted to thank you for last night," Hanna announced as she slipped the key in the lock. "I hope you're not too afraid to try it again."

"No, I'd love to." Tianna felt bad for lying. She really liked Hanna.

"Thank you," Hanna answered softly, and worked the key. Then she pushed open the door.

"You're a lifesaver, Hanna." Tianna felt like giving her a kiss, but instead she hurried into the room.

"You'd better keep it." Hanna tried to hand her the key.

Tianna smiled. "I won't be needing it again. I promise."

"Then I'm off." Hanna turned and started toward the stairs. "See you tonight," she called back.

"Yeah," Tianna answered sadly, and shut the door.

She quickly slipped into the clean underwear from her backpack and had started pulling on the same clothes she had worn yesterday when a scratching sound made her stop. She looked around, expecting to see a mouse or a squirrel that somehow had gotten into the room from the tree.

But what she saw made her freeze in terror. She watched with alarm as the letter *H* slowly appeared on the wall above the dresser. Something or someone was writing a message. Instinct told her it wasn't a ghost. It was someone or something trying to communicate with her from that other realm.

Slowly the words *Help me I'm Catty* appeared on the wall.

Catty must be the girl she had seen. The name was unusual. It had to be Vanessa's friend, the one Michael had told her about who had disappeared. Could she have somehow been trapped in that other dimension? It had to be.

Then another scraping sound made her tense. As she stared at the first message other words were scrawled over it. *Stay away.*

CHAPTER FIFTEEN

FOR A MOMENT TIANNA sat dumbfounded, unable to move. She couldn't leave Los Angeles even if it was dangerous for her to stay. She had to help Catty. She wouldn't be able to live with herself if she ran away now because she would always know she had been a coward. She had to act even if she failed. She dressed rapidly, grabbed up her backpack, and hurried outside, her hair still wet against her back.

Derek looked up, surprised. He was sitting on the steps. "That was fast."

She walked right past him. "Hurry," she commanded.

He stood and started following her.

"Give me the keys," she ordered.

"You want to drive?" he asked.

"I'll get us to school faster," she said as she opened the driver's-side door and tossed a stack of travel magazines into the back.

"I brought the magazines for you to look at," Derek complained.

"Later." She held out her hand for the keys.

He hesitated. "Do you have a driver's license?"

"Of course," she said, not knowing if it was true or not. She was already sitting behind the steering wheel.

He tossed her the keys and she turned the ignition as he climbed into the car.

She pressed hard on the gas pedal and the car shrieked away from the curb. The back end fishtailed. She needed to get to school quickly and find some answers. She had a feeling that Catty wasn't going to last long in that place.

The light turned yellow ahead of her.

"Slow down!" Derek shouted as the car in front of them stopped for the light.

She didn't let up.

"You're going to rear-end it!" Derek cried, and his foot pressed the floor as if he were trying to work an invisible brake.

She jerked the steering wheel, swerved smoothly around the car, and blasted through the intersection, ignoring the flurry of horns and screeching tires.

Derek snapped his seat belt in place. "Why are you in such a hurry to get to school?"

"Geometry test," she answered, and buzzed around two more cars.

At the next junction she needed to make a left-hand turn, but the line of traffic waiting for the green arrow would delay her too long. She continued in her lane, and when she reached the intersection, she turned in front of the car with the right-of-way. Angry honks followed her as she blasted onto the next street.

"We've got time, Tianna!" Derek yelled. "School doesn't start for another fifteen minutes."

Would fifteen minutes give her enough time to get the answers she needed? She didn't think so.

She pressed her foot harder on the accelerator. The school was at least a mile away, but if she ignored the next light and the next, then maybe she could get there with enough time to question Corrine. She didn't think her powers were strong enough to change the lights and she didn't want to chance endangering other drivers, but she was sure she could at least slow down the cross traffic.

She concentrated on the cars zooming east and west on Beverly Boulevard in front of her without slowing her speed.

"Tianna!" Derek yelled. "You've got a red light!"

She squinted and stalled a Jaguar in the crosswalk. Cars honked impatiently behind the car, and when a Toyota tried to speed around it, she stopped it, too. She could feel the pressure building inside her as she made a Range Rover and a pick-up slide to a halt. She shot through the busy intersection against the light.

Derek turned back. "You've got to be the luckiest person in the world."

"Right," she answered with a smirk. "I have the worst luck of anyone you can imagine."

"You?" he asked in disbelief.

"Me," she answered, and glanced in the rearview mirror. Traffic had started to flow down Beverly Boulevard again.

She sped around the corner in a tight turn.

"We're here," she said, and pressed hard on the horn to let kids in the parking lot know she was coming through.

She parked with a jerk and slammed on the brakes.

Derek bounced forward, then back. He turned and looked at her with shock in his eyes. "Where'd you learn to drive?"

"I made it up as I went along." She opened the car door and tossed him the keys. "Thanks for the lift, Derek." She grabbed her backpack and ran.

She didn't recognize Corrine at first, sitting outside the geometry classroom, legs stretched in front of her, doing some last minute cramming. She wasn't wearing makeup and her eyes looked clear, her skin fresh and beautiful.

"You look good." Tianna squatted beside her. "Tell me about Catty."

Corrine stared at her briefly, surprised, then she nervously looked around her as if she were afraid to speak. Finally she closed her geometry book and began. "I was there that night at Planet Bang," Corrine whispered. "When this girl came running inside. I didn't know who she was, but she was asking for Vanessa, Catty, Serena, and Jimena. She found them and they all went charging outside. Twenty minutes later they're back, minus Catty, and you could tell something was really wrong. They hid in the bathroom, except Jimena, who was all tough and lying for them."

"What do you mean, lying for them?" Tianna asked.

"When the police questioned them," Corrine confided. "She told the police they hadn't gone outside, but they had. I saw them. I was too afraid to say anything."

She paused as if something had made her hesitate. Tianna glanced up. Serena, Jimena, and

Vanessa were walking down the hall toward them.

"Go on," Tianna urged.

Corrine's voice was lower now. "A few blocks away all these fires had broken out and there were fire engines and police cars and all the people in the neighborhood were saying that teenagers had been playing with firecrackers and explosives."

"Is that what you think?" Tianna asked.

Corinne shook her head, and her eyes never left Serena, Jimena, and Vanessa. "I don't think it was explosives. I think the fireworks were from some kind of magical power because they never found Catty's body. I think they did something to her."

"Like what?" Tianna felt tense.

Corrine turned and looked at her. "I think they killed her."

"How?" Tianna glanced back at Serena, Jimena, and Vanessa. They might act strange, but she definitely knew they weren't capable of murder.

"I think they cast a spell and it went wrong."

Corrine finished. "There, I've said too much already."

Could Corrine be right? Maybe they were witches and they had cast a spell. But that didn't feel right. Modern witches, like wiccans, were loving and kind. It was only superstition and misunderstanding that made people think they used their charms malevolently.

She wondered if they could have done something to their friend. Maybe it had started out as fun, but a fatal mistake had been made. Then another terrifying thought came to her. Maybe they weren't witches at all but kids who dabbled with magic of a darker kind. Did they have power enough to conjure up a demon? Was that what the shadow had been?

Tianna needed her memories back now more than ever. If she could go into that other realm, then there must be something she could do to help Catty, but what? If she could only remember.

Corrine touched her arm and she jumped.

"Are you all right?" Corrine looked worried.

Tianna nodded.

"Can I borrow a pencil for the test?" she asked. "I forgot mine."

"Sure." Tianna opened her backpack and saw the diary. With everything that had been going on yesterday, she had completely forgotten about it. Now she'd have some answers. Her heart beat fast with anticipation. Maybe she'd even learn about that other dimension and then she could find a way to help Catty.

She handed Corrine the pencil and stood. "See ya."

"You'll miss the test," Corrine called after her.

"Like I care," Tianna muttered. She charged down the hallway, then ran across the blacktop to the metal detectors. She didn't want some hall monitor snooping around and sending her back to class. The best thing to do was to leave campus. The security guards at the front gate were too busy checking purses and backpacks to notice anyone running back outside.

As soon as she was away from the campus, she stood near the curb and started to read.

The social worker claims I ran away again. Of course, I didn't. Mason and Justin found me, so I had no choice but to leave. They almost caught me, too. They're getting closer. Time is running out—

Before she could read more, a hand grabbed the diary away.

CHAPTER SIXTEEN

TIANNA TURNED QUICKLY to see who had stolen her diary.

Derek opened it, then glanced up at her with a sly smile. "Does it say anything about me?"

"Give it back." She leaned her head to the side and started walking toward him with her hand outstretched.

"I want to see if you're as good at keep away as you are at soccer," he teased.

"I'm not in the mood," she snapped, and charged after him. She leaped for the diary as he started to hand it back, and accidentally knocked it from his hand. It skidded across the sidewalk. She tried to use her power to stop it before it slid into the street, but she was too flustered, and instead she made the gutter water slosh against the curb and slop onto the sidewalk.

She dove into the oncoming traffic, trying to retrieve it.

Derek grabbed her arm and pulled her back as a huge UPS truck rolled over the diary and smashed its binding. Pages soared in a circle, then fell into a pothole filled with muddy water.

"That could have been you under the truck wheel," Derek said. "What's wrong with you, anyway? I was going to hand it back to you. You're acting like it was a matter of life or death."

"It was." She sighed and watched the wet pages flap and tear apart as car after car whizzed by and rolled over what might have been her life. She could use her power to bring the pages back, but they would be unreadable now.

She and Derek fell into a strained silence. Then he spoke. "Why did you run away from me back at the parking lot?"

"Geometry test," she mumbled, and watched the soggy pages become no more than a soft, pulpy mass under the steady stream of tires.

"For someone so worried about her geometry test, you've already missed the first bell." He looked at her. "Why did you lie to me?"

"You'd never understand." She shook her head. What was she going to do? That was her only chance of finding a way to save Catty. Her only hope now was to get her memories back. No chance of that.

Derek started to say something and she stopped him.

"Derek, I just need some time alone, okay?"

"I think we need to talk." There was a seriousness in his eyes that she didn't understand.

"Not now." She started walking away from him. She hadn't gone half the block when footsteps ran after her and someone grabbed her shoulder.

"Derek," she said angrily. "I need to be alone." She turned with a scowl.

Michael stood behind her.

"Hi, Michael." She hoped there wasn't too much eagerness on her face. Just looking into his dark gentle eyes made her feel better.

"Were you looking for Derek?" His lips curled in an infectious smile.

"No." She grinned foolishly. "Are you cutting school today?" And then she added too quickly, assuming that he was, "Want to hang out?"

"I don't start until second period," he explained.

"Oh." She didn't bother to hide her disappointment. She would have loved some time alone with him.

"I saw you walking and I wanted to remind you about Planet Bang tonight." He stepped closer.

Her hands went automatically to his chest and played with his shirt button. "I'll be there." She looked at his lips. She bet he was a great kisser, and she was determined to find out for herself. She breathed deeply and took in his spicy aftershave. What would he do if she put her arms around him right here and pulled his face down to hers? She looked up at him, wondering if she could use her power to bend his will to hers.

"See you tonight, then." He pulled away. Was there promise in his eyes, or had that only been her imagination?

She watched him walk toward school. She loved the way his black hair fell in curls around his neck. She sighed. Michael was the only thing going right in her life. No matter what else happened, she was resolved to have some fun tonight. She was going to get that kiss. She didn't care how bold she had to be.

But first she had to do something.

CHAPTER SEVENTEEN

TIANNA CREPT THROUGH a patch of ivy and hid in the shadows near a stone wall. It was past dusk, and cars were pulling into driveways. She watched with yearning as children raced up to porches to escape the cool air, their backpacks and school papers clasped in their hands. Soon the dark windows swam with warm golden lights and acrid smoke filled the air from hearth fires in the homes up and down the street. She stared at the thin gray wisps circling from the chimneys and envied the people who lived inside. She imagined them cozy in front of blazing flames.

Her eyes went back to the two-story Tudor home. It stood alone, back from the street, its entry porch dark. The windows indifferently stared back at her, reflecting the amber color from the streetlamps.

She didn't think Mason or Justin lived there, but she prayed whoever did might have the answers she needed. A car turned the corner. The beams from its headlights swept over her. She pressed back into darkness as it spun into the drive of the Tudor home and the automatic garage door opened. The car went inside and the door slowly closed after it.

With quick, even steps Tianna crossed the street. She didn't go up the front walk but to the side of the house. She glanced behind her. If anyone happened to look out their window and see her, they would think her movements were furtive and probably call the police.

She scurried into the shadows along a wall and crept to the back, then scaled the fence and fell into the yard of the Tudor house, trampling a bed of red gladiolas. She hurried around a swimming pool, shaded by Mexican fan palms, then stepped quickly across a long patio crowded with potted plants.

Her breath was too loud now. She waited until it came in slow, even draws again. Then she found a rock and hit the plastic covering on the sliding door latch. She wondered how she knew so much about breaking and entering, but she never questioned what her hands were doing. She had discovered in the past two days that if she didn't think and just let her body act, there were a lot of surprising things she could do.

When the plastic cover fell to the patio floor, her fingers released a metal hook inside. One click and the Tudor home was no longer safe from an intruder.

She paused, nerves on end, then as silently as she could she slid back the door and entered. A television played cartoons loudly somewhere in the house. She stole her way across the dark family room to the lit kitchen and peeked secretively inside.

A woman in pink slacks and a white sweater

spooned ground coffee into a coffeepot. A young girl of about twelve with a bald head and swollen face stared into an open refrigerator. Behind her a thin boy in a wheelchair rolled to the table and spread peanut butter onto cut pieces of celery.

The girl took an apple, and as she closed the refrigerator door, their eyes met. "Tianna!" Her smile was huge. She dropped the apple and ran to her, arms spread wide.

Tianna stepped into the kitchen, baffled, and embraced the young girl.

"I knew you'd come back," the girl said.

The boy grabbed the gear on his wheelchair. Its motor whirred and he twirled around, his smile crooked but his happiness showing through.

Then the woman shot a worried glance at Tianna, and her forehead wrinkled as if seeing her had brought on sudden distress. "Thank God you're all right."

Tianna blinked. "Mom?"

"Mom?" the girl repeated, and laughed.

The woman patiently hushed her. Then she turned to Tianna. "You can call me that if you want." She put a cautionary finger to Tianna's lips. "But don't say anything more."

"Is the house bugged?" Tianna asked.

"I wish it were that simple," the woman explained. "They can read minds."

Her answer sent a chill through Tianna. "You know?"

"Now I do. I didn't believe you, either, at first, but then they came here." She looked at Tianna with mounting concern. "What happened? No, don't tell me." She shook her head. "If I know, they'll find out. I can't stop them from getting inside my head."

"I don't remember anything," Tianna confessed. "I know I should know you, but I don't."

"They must have done something to you." The woman didn't act as if Tianna's confession was strange at all. "I'm Mary, and this is Shannon."

"You really don't remember?" Shannon asked.

Tianna shook her head.

"And Todd." Mary smiled lovingly at the boy.

"You didn't forget me, did you?" Todd waved. "We played Monopoly."

"Sorry." Tianna shrugged.

"Sit down." Mary pulled out a chair. "I'll tell you everything I know, but it's not a lot." That look of fear shot across her face again. "I don't think they'll come back now, but if they do, run. Don't worry about us. It's you they want."

"How do you know?" Tianna felt Shannon's comforting hand on her arm.

"Because when they go into your mind to read," Mary explained, "they leave a residue of themselves. I can't say how I know, but I do."

Tianna sat down. Her knees felt too weak to hold her any longer, and her fingers began trembling.

Shannon took her hand and squeezed it tightly. "We're here for you, Tianna. We're family now, just like Mary said."

"You were an emergency placement—" Mary began.

"Placement?" Tianna asked.

"I'm a foster mother," Mary explained.

"I have no home?" Tianna felt her heart drop, but it wasn't as much of a shock as it should have been. Part of her had known she had been running for a long time. Still, she had hoped.

"I'm sorry," Mary answered with true concern. "They called me two weeks ago and asked if I could take . . ." She stopped.

"What?" Tianna asked, wondering if there was something wrong with her.

Mary regarded her kindly. "The social worker wanted to know if there was any way I could handle a problem teen."

Tianna waited for Mary to explain.

"She said you kept running away from your placement homes and she thought maybe I could make a difference because I had been so successful with others in the past."

Tianna knew immediately that there was something Mary wasn't saying. "So the kids and I went shopping and got everything for your room," Mary continued. "We were excited to have one more in our home."

That explained one mystery at least, Tianna

thought. Now she knew why the decor and her style of clothes were so different.

"And then you arrived." Mary brushed back a strand of hair that had fallen into her face.

"In a really bad mood," Shannon added.

"Yeah." Todd rolled his eyes.

"Sorry," Tianna whispered.

"You had no clothes, no personal belongings," Mary remarked. "You said everything had been stolen. So we went shopping. You have great taste, by the way."

Tianna smiled.

"It seemed like everything was going to be fine," Mary went on. "But then, you became nervous and kept checking the locks. That didn't seem too odd, considering we live in L.A. Twice during the night on Sunday you woke me up but it was as if you were checking to make sure I was okay. I had been home-schooling you so I thought maybe it would help if you went to high school and made some friends."

The coffeepot gurgled and the smell of freshly brewed coffee filled the room.

"Would you like a cup?" Mary asked as she stood and poured herself one.

Tianna shook her head.

Mary sat down and took a sip before she continued. "Monday morning I enrolled you in La Brea High, and then I took the kids over to the hospital for their treatments. When we got home, you were already waiting for us. You told me that the two guys who had been chasing you were back. I wanted to call the police, but you told me not to. You said the police department had never believed you before. I called them, anyway, of course."

Tianna thought of the note in her shoe. "And they didn't believe me this time, either, did they?"

"You told them the guys had big shining yellow eyes," Shannon put in. "Nobody believed you. Not even me."

"Me neither." Todd shook his head.

"I felt sad that such an athletic and intelligent girl like you had lost touch with reality again. The social worker had told me that you had delusions. But then . . ." Mary looked at the children, and Tianna could feel their fear. "Tuesday night we found out it wasn't a delusion at all. Everything you said was true."

"How?" Tianna was worried now that Justin and Mason might come back and hurt them.

"You had gone to Planet Bang. Maybe I shouldn't have let you, but you seemed to like this boy so much and I thought it would be helpful for you to get out with . . ."

"Normal kids," Tianna finished the sentence for her.

Mary's eyes looked sad as she nodded. "There was a horrible pounding on the front door."

"Like someone was trying to break it down." Shannon's eyes widened.

"I thought something had happened to you," Mary said. "I swung open the door and two boys a little older than you were standing on the porch. They were evil. I have no other explanation for the strange feeling they gave to the air around them. They looked at me, and I could feel them prowling inside my mind. They were trying to find you."

"Their eyes were glowing yellow, too," Todd said interrupting. "Just like you told the cops."

Mary nodded. "They read my mind and ran off to Planet Bang to find you. We got in the car as quickly as we could and drove over to warn you."

Todd made a noise imitating a jet plane.

"But you were gone when we got there," Mary went on. "I didn't tell the social worker or the police about the two boys. I knew they wouldn't believe me, either. I barely believed it myself. I just prayed that you had gotten away. We would have run, too, but we couldn't. Shannon and Todd needed to go to Children's Hospital for their treatments."

"We all slept together in my room." Todd made a face. "Shannon snores."

"I do not," she argued, and slapped at him playfully.

"You weren't scared?" Tianna asked, and then felt foolish. It looked as if Shannon and Todd were facing death every day from other sources.

"Of course they weren't as frightened as I

was," Mary said proudly. "They are extremely brave."

Tianna looked at Mary. "Did they come back?"

She nodded. "The next day. I'm not sure why. When we came home, the front door was open and they had broken a vase in the upstairs hallway. Odd—why that vase?"

Tianna didn't bother to explain that she had done it accidentally.

"They came back that night," Mary continued. "They seemed angry that there was nothing new to dig from my mind. I was thinking that I should take the children to a hotel, but then I overheard the one with all the piercings say it was going to be over soon, so I decided to stay."

"Do you know what the *it* was?"

Mary shook her head. "Sorry, I don't have any idea. Although . . ."

"What?" Tianna leaned forward.

"It's not based on anything. It's more a feeling I had after they left my mind."

Tianna nodded.

"They were trying to stop you from doing something, and if they could hold you off for just one more night, it would be too late for you to do anything."

Tianna wondered what it could be. If only she had her memories. She stood and scraped back the chair. She liked Shannon and Todd and Mary. She wished they really were her family.

"Well, I'd better go." Then she remembered the clothes upstairs. She needed something to wear to Planet Bang. It didn't sound as if she was going to live long, anyway, so she might as well enjoy the little time she had, and more than anything she wanted that kiss from Michael.

"Can I take some of the clothes?" Tianna asked.

"Of course," Mary answered. "They're all yours. Take anything you need."

CHAPTER EIGHTEEN

AN HOUR LATER Tianna was walking toward Planet Bang, wearing a sweater shell with sequins and an ankle-grazing skirt slit up the sides to the top of her thighs. She glanced at the waning moon and stopped. There was something important she had to do before the moon turned dark and it was in some way connected to Justin and Mason, but what? She stared at the sky as she continued, hoping the memory would come to her the way soccer and skateboarding had.

When she rounded the corner, the music grew louder. A neon sign throbbed pink, blue, green, and orange lights over the kids waiting to go inside. She recognized some of them. It seemed as if everyone had come with a friend or friends. Their heads turned and watched her as she walked to the end of the line.

She spread her hands through her hair and arched her back. As long as they were going to stare, she might as well give them a show. She twisted her body and stuck one long leg out from the slit in her skirt. Guys smiled back at her as she stretched her arms in a sexy pose. The girls mostly turned away, pretending they hadn't been checking out their competition.

The music coming from inside excited her. She could hear kids whoop and stomp in time to the beat. She couldn't wait to dance. She wanted that at least, especially if it meant dancing with Michael. She breathed out, trying to calm herself. If only . . . Life could be so perfect here. She tried not to think about Mason and Justin, but her eyes nervously scanned the nearby shadows anyway and she wished the line would move faster.

Finally it was her turn with the security

guards. She handed her backpack to the first one. He smiled at her, and there was no doubt in her mind it was intended as a flirt. He couldn't have been much older than she was. His hands went rapidly through her things.

"What are you doing?" he joked when he saw her underwear. "It looks like you carry your whole life in here."

"I do," she answered with a tilt of her head, then she took her bag and went inside.

She liked the feel of energy that was coming off the crowd. Lights flashed and shimmery clothes sparkled around the room. Girls wore full-on body glitter and some had diamond-sparkle tattoos on their faces and arms. She set her backpack on the floor in the corner near bags, sweaters, jackets, and shoes.

The music beat through her and she started to dance, her eyes searching for Michael. She found Michelle instead, leaning on crutches, her foot in a cast. She wore slacks with cutouts on the side that revealed the bare tan skin of her hips and thighs. Her hair was in ringlets clasped back with diamonds away from her face.

Tianna walked over to her. "Great outfit. I like your hair, too."

Michelle jerked back and almost tripped.

Tianna caught her. "I'm sorry about your ankle."

"Stay away from me," Michelle warned, and hobbled away.

Tianna saw Corrine on the other side of the floor and waved. She wore a funky tiara with stars and only a little makeup. Tianna had started to push through the crowd toward her when a hand touched her back. She turned, hoping to stare up into Michael's beautiful eyes, but instead Vanessa, Serena, and Jimena circled her.

"Hi," Tianna said, and pushed through their circle. She had other plans for the night, and it didn't include being with witches. She shoved into the crowd and started to dance.

Jimena twirled after her with a laugh.

"We overheard you talking to Corrine about Catty." Jimena spoke above the music. She was wearing big hoop earrings and a sequined mesh dress with gold sandals.

Tianna knew she was lying. She couldn't have overheard her talking to Corrine. They had been whispering, and Jimena and her friends had been too far away.

"So?" Tianna answered, wondering if she could get more information from them about Catty. She glided beside Jimena, hips touching hips, enjoying the way Jimena danced.

"We didn't exactly hear you," Serena confessed. "We found out another way."

Tianna wondered who had spied on her. Derek hadn't been around. The only other person would have been Corrine herself, but she seemed too frightened by them to say anything and Serena had been too far away to read her mind, or had she?

Suddenly Vanessa stepped in front of her. She wore a spaghetti-strapped red dress, with a red leather jacket over her shoulders.

"We'd like to know why you were asking about her," Vanessa said. "That's all."

Tianna didn't think they'd believe her if she did tell them why she had been asking about Catty. Besides, she had questions of her own. "I just wanted to hear what happened the night Catty disappeared." She watched them closely to see if there was any reaction, and there definitely had been one in Vanessa's eyes. "Maybe you should tell me."

Vanessa stepped closer. "Is there a reason why it's important to you?"

Jimena stopped dancing and stood beside her, arms folded over her chest with determination. "Something happened to our friend, and if you know anything, we'd like to hear it."

Tianna stopped dancing and looked back at her. She didn't like the strange way Serena was staring at her.

"Don't believe everything you hear at school about us or Catty," Serena warned. "We're not witches, and we can't cast spells."

"Who said you could?" Tianna answered defensively.

"More than anything we want to get Catty

back," Vanessa put in. "We really miss her. If you know anything, please tell us."

Her statement surprised Tianna. That didn't sound as if they thought Catty was dead. She wondered if they knew their friend was trapped in another world. "Then tell me what happened that night." Her eyes held a dare and she waited for Vanessa's reply, but before she could answer, warm hands touched Tianna's shoulder and pulled her away. She turned and looked up into Michael's eyes.

His hands smoothed down her bare arms to her wrists, making a pleasant ache spread through her.

"I was hoping I'd find you." He guided her deeper into the crowd away from Vanessa, Jimena, and Serena.

When he stopped, she lifted her hands over her head and started to dance, teasing him. Her hips moved sultry and slow, the beat of the song echoing her intense desire. He smiled as if he knew she was playing with him. Then his arms circled her waist. Sweet anticipation spread through her, and she brought her hands down slowly and entwined them around his neck.

"I'm glad you came," he said at last.

"Me, too." She inched closer until she could feel the movement of his leg against her thigh.

He bent down, his face close to hers. She liked the feel of his breath against her neck. She closed her eyes and let her lips rest on his cheek.

"Normally I don't get into matchmaking," he said into her ear.

She pulled back abruptly. "Excuse me?"

"I think you and Derek make a great couple." He smiled at her as if he were embarrassed for being so bold. He seemed to sense her confusion. "I was hoping you'd give Derek another chance."

"Did I ever give him a first one?" She glanced over Michael's shoulder and saw Derek staring back at her.

"He's got a big crush on you, and it did seem as if you liked him until Wednesday," Michael explained. "What happened?"

"Derek?" She looked back into Michael's beautiful eyes. Was that the only reason Michael had been so affectionate? For Derek? She felt heartsick.

"Did you talk to Tianna yet?" Vanessa suddenly stood next to them and started dancing, her body sinuous and easy.

Michael nodded.

"You and Derek are good together," Vanessa added. She looked so sincere.

Tianna wished she'd smirk or give her the slightest reason to hate her. She wanted to, but she couldn't. Vanessa was too genuine and good for anyone to dislike.

Someone tapped her shoulder. She slumped. She didn't even need to look behind her to know who it was. She sadly watched as Michael pulled Vanessa close to him and they danced away.

At last she turned.

"Hi," Derek said, his eyes sparkling with optimism. "I hope you don't mind that I had Michael speak for me."

She glanced back at the dancers. Michael caught her looking at him and gave her a thumbs-up.

"I thought everything was going so well until Wednesday." Derek put his hand tentatively on her waist. "Then you acted like you didn't even know me. I didn't understand. I thought we'd hooked up."

"Yeah, well, things happened." She looked at him. She knew he'd never believe her even if she did tell him that she woke up that day and couldn't remember her own name.

"Let's dance." He pulled her to him.

She stared into his eyes. He was sweet and likable. She'd never hurt his feelings, but he was no Michael Saratoga. She glanced over his shoulder, but Vanessa and Michael were gone now.

"You know, I don't feel very well," Tianna said, and made a mental promise to herself that if she got through this night, she would never lie again. "I've got a headache."

"Are you getting headaches since that hit you took in soccer?" He looked concerned.

"Yeah, from the soccer hit." She started to pull away.

He squeezed through the dancers after her.

"You'd better see a doctor," he suggested. "I'll give you a ride home."

"It's all right." She stopped at the door. "I can walk. I don't want to take you away from the fun."

But he had already left the building without getting his hand stamped. He kept glancing down at her legs as they peeked out from beneath her skirt.

She sighed. In trying to get away from him she had left her backpack inside. She started to ask him to go back and get it for her, but he spoke first.

"I'm sorry about the way I treated your cousins the last time we were here. I thought maybe that's why you were upset with me."

"What cousins?" She put her hands on her hips and studied him.

"Those weird punker dudes." He shrugged. "It's hard to imagine they're related to you, but they said—"

"Derek, what are you talking about?" She was getting a real headache now. A strange buzzing in her head made her squint.

"I just felt bad about the way I treated them," Derek replied. "I didn't know they were related to you. They explained everything to me when I saw them at Starbucks today."

It dawned on her. "Mason and Justin?"

"Yeah. I told them you'd be here tonight." He smiled and pointed. "There they are."

Justin and Mason slowly walked toward her. Their eyes flashed with red and gold sparks as if a fire burned inside their heads.

"They're not my cousins, Derek." She needed to do something and fast, but she didn't want Derek to see her use her power. Somehow she felt that the less he knew, the safer he would be. The best thing to do was flee. She started to run, but Derek grabbed her hand and stopped her.

She turned and stared into Derek's eyes. They seemed triumphant. Was he one of them?

CHAPTER NINETEEN

TIANNA WOKE UP AND blinked. She was lying on her side, arms behind her, face pressed against a cold, damp concrete floor. Slowly, thin bars of pale orange light came into focus on the wall above her. It looked like the outline of a door. Another grayish glow to her left appeared to be a dirt-streaked window. She must be in a cellar. That explained the foul odor of mold and mildew.

She couldn't remember how she had gotten here, but at least she still had the memories of who had captured her. Justin and Mason wanted her for something. She was sure they had kidnapped her so they could turn her into one of them. Her chest tightened as her apprehension deepened. What were they?

Then she recalled how Derek had stopped her before she could escape. She wondered if he had always been part of their group. He had seemed like such a nice guy.

A scuttling noise made her heart drop. It sounded like tiny feet dragging a long skinny tail. She hated rats, and she wasn't waiting until one was in her face; she was leaving now. She tried to move, but something stopped her.

"No," she moaned. Her hands and legs were tied. She stretched her fingers and felt the ropes and knots binding her wrists, then concentrated her telekinetic powers to loosen them.

"Tianna?"

"Derek?" Her head jerked around. She couldn't see anything but shadow.

"Are you down here, too?" His voice seemed shaky.

"Yes." She tried to sound calm to reassure him.

"Those dripping water sounds are driving me crazy," he complained.

She listened. She hadn't noticed the constant ping and drip of water coming from the corner. "Yeah, I guess it would have bothered me, too, but I just woke up." She hadn't been sleeping, exactly, but it was close enough to the truth. Her mind continued working on loosening the knots that held the ropes around her wrists.

"I thought I was alone." His relief was obvious.

She was grateful he wasn't in league with Mason and Justin, but at the same time her heart sank. It was going to be harder to escape now. She would have to protect Derek. Then she remembered that her last thought before blacking out had been that he had betrayed her. So what was he doing here?

"Why did you stop me when I tried to run away?" she asked, not bothering to hide the accusation in her tone. She felt the ropes loosen and now tried to uncoil them with her mental energy.

"I thought you should speak to your

cousins," he explained in an embarrassed voice. "But I guess they weren't your cousins after all."

"How could you think they were?" She started to scold him but stopped. Anger was a waste of time, and she needed to conserve her energy.

"I'm sorry I believed their story about your family squabble. I swear I thought I was bridging a gap so you could all be together for Thanksgiving. I didn't know it would end up like this."

"It's all right," she sighed.

"I should have been suspicious," he countered. "I'm such a dunderhead."

"No, you're not," she reassured him.

"But I knew better," Derek insisted, "I saw what they were doing Tuesday night, and then I went ahead and believed their story. They said you were stubborn." He stopped, and when he continued, there was a light tease in his voice. "Okay, maybe that part of their story is true."

"Thanks," she answered sarcastically as the ropes around her wrists dropped free. She brought her hands in front of her. They prickled painfully as the blood flowed back to the tips of her fingers. She shook them, and when they were no longer numb, she examined the ropes around her ankles.

"What did they do to me?" she asked. "Why was I unconscious?"

"You won't believe me if I tell you," he answered.

"Right now, I'd believe anything," she assured him. "You can't begin to imagine everything I've seen in the last two days."

"Their eyes turned yellow," he answered finally. "And they used them to make you pass out."

When she didn't laugh, he continued. "You don't think it was my imagination?" He didn't wait for her to answer. "You know about them. What are they? Something supernatural? They look it. So tell me."

"I wish I knew," she answered as the first knot tying her ankles came loose.

"Maybe they escaped from a genetics lab? I mean, you see it in the movies all the time— maybe the government really is working on some kind of superhuman." He took in a deep breath and was silent for a moment as if considering what he was going to say next. "Do you think they're Martians?"

"Martians?"

"You know, guys from outer space. They can . . ." He started, then stopped as if he was still in awe of what he had seen.

"What?"

"Talk right in your head." Derek let out a long breath. "I know you can't believe me—"

"But I do," she answered bluntly.

"You do?" He seemed relieved.

"Yes, they've been chasing me for a long time, and somehow on Tuesday night they stole my memories."

She could hear him moving as if he was try-ing to get closer to her. "That's why you acted so strange Wednesday morning at school?"

"Yes."

He was silent a moment. "And you're not really a runaway. I mean, you are, but you have a reason to be on the run."

"I guess I've been running for a long time." She felt sad and quickly changed the subject. "Did you hear anything that could help us?"

"Yeah, I overheard them on the car ride over." He stopped as if something had suddenly baffled him.

"What?" she asked, sensing it was important.

"They're waiting for a third guy to show up so they can take us down to the beach. They're going to cross us over, whatever that means."

"I know it can't be anything good," Tianna answered.

He sighed. "There's no way to escape, so I guess we'll find out."

"How can you be such a pessimist?"

"We're both tied up," he answered. "The ropes are too tight. I've been trying to loosen them, but they won't budge."

"They didn't tie me up," she lied. She figured he couldn't have seen her working the ropes in the dark, anyway.

"They didn't tie you up?" He sounded surprised.

"I guess they thought I'd remain unconscious."

"Untie me, then," he urged.

"All right." She stood and tripped over something in the dark, then stumbled and fell on Derek.

"Ouch," he moaned.

"Are you all right?" she whispered, and realized she was lying on top of him. She liked the way his body felt so familiar and comfortable beneath hers. She rested her head against his chest and closed her eyes, suddenly regretting all the mean things she had said to him.

"Aren't you going to get up?" he asked.

"Sure," she answered, and let her hands smooth down his chest and then his arms. She was surprised by the feel of his rock-hard muscles.

"I work out," he murmured unexpectedly.

"What?"

He snickered. "The way you're feeling my chest and arms—"

"I am not." She jumped up, indignant, then knelt beside him. "I was searching for your ropes."

"Liar," he whispered.

She felt a blush rise to her cheeks and was glad it was dark so he couldn't see.

"The ropes are tied around my ankles and wrists," he said, but there was still laughter in his voice.

Her fingers traveled down his jeans leg and found the rope. The knots were too tight. It would take her forever if she picked at them. Instead she imagined the coils wiggling free. Within moments she tossed the ropes aside.

Derek stretched his legs. "Thanks. Get my hands."

She pushed a stack of boxes aside, then felt the ropes that held his hands behind his back. The tips of her fingers touched his palm and lingered there as if they had memories of their own.

"Is there a problem?" he asked.

"No, why?" she answered, not wanting to take her hand away.

"Just that you're taking so long."

She used her telekinetic powers to undo the ropes. As soon as his hands were free, he waved them in the dark, searching for her.

"You okay?" he asked. His fingers brushed across her cheek and settled lightly on her chin. He leaned closer. She drew in air. His warm breath caressed her lips.

"Come on," he whispered. "We've got to get out of here." He grabbed her hand and helped her stand.

She wondered if she would have let him kiss her if he had tried. She didn't understand her disappointment that he hadn't. She liked Michael, didn't she?

Then she froze. Hollow footsteps pounded on the floorboards overhead.

"They're on the move," he said cautioning her.

"Do you think they heard us?" She used that as an excuse to put her arms around him.

"It sounds like they're going outside." He started forward again.

The distant sound of a door opening and closing came to them.

"Yes, definitely they went outside," Derek said. "Hurry, let's get to the stairs.

"Stairs?" She followed him blindly through puddles and over stacks of wood and pipes.

"Since the door is up so high," he explained, "there must be stairs."

"Yes," she answered with a sudden rush of excitement. If they could get up to the door, she could use her powers to open it. She hurried after him.

"That's odd." He seemed perplexed. "They must have removed the stairs."

"Why?" She waved her hands in front of her, searching. Nothing was there. Not even a ladder.

She sat down on the floor in total frustration. That's why Justin and Mason had been so careless. Even if she had come to and used her power to untie her ropes, there was no way she was going to get up to the door. She couldn't fly. "There must be another entrance. How did they get us down here?"

Derek was silent for too long.

"What's wrong?" she asked.

"Do you think it's possible that they took

away some of my memories?" He seemed distressed. "I remember the car pulling up out front and the next thing I recall is being tied up alone in the basement, but I don't remember how I got down here and I don't remember them bringing you down here, either."

"Anything's possible." She stood and touched the wall. Water seeped over the bricks. Then her fingers felt something marshy and soft. Her hands jerked back. "Yuck."

"What now?"

"The wall. It's covered with some kind of creepy mold. It feels totally gross." She wiped her hands down her skirt.

"We're in a basement." He laughed. "I didn't think you'd be so squeamish."

"You touch it," she said.

She heard him shuffle forward.

"Jeez. What is this stuff?"

She took off her shoes and handed them to him.

"What are you doing now?" he asked.

"I'm getting us out."

"How?"

She didn't like the disbelief in his voice.

"I'm going to scale the wall." Already her mind's eye had started working a brick to make it stick out a few inches so she would have something to step onto. A soft squishy grating noise let her know she had been successful.

"What was that?" Derek asked.

"What?"

"That sound."

"My hands slipped," she explained. "I'm trying to find protruding bricks." That was partly true. She ran her fingers along the wall. The mold and moisture made the bricks slippery, and even after forcing them out at an angle the surfaces were hard to grip.

Derek stood next to her. "You think you can do it?" he asked hopefully. "Be careful."

"I will." Her fingers grabbed hold of another ice-cold slimy brick. She paused to make sure she had a strong hold, then felt with her foot for something to step on. It was worse feeling the gummy mildew squish between her toes. She had to struggle for balance until she could find another brick.

A few minutes later she was almost there. All she had to do now was use her power to open the door, then climb onto the floor and help Derek out. She clasped the jutting edges tightly, her fingers slipping, and concentrated on moving another brick out. A sludgy scraping sound followed, and a glop of squashy stuff fell on her face.

"Yuck," she moaned.

She blinked, then reached up and felt along the wall for a brick that was sticking out. She wrapped her fingers around it and too late realized it was completely covered with spongy mold. Her fingers slid off and she fell back, plunging to the basement floor.

CHAPTER TWENTY

DEREK TRIED TO BREAK her fall but only succeeded in tumbling to the basement floor with her. Tianna landed on her back, her head hit the concrete. Hot pain rushed through her skull with the roar of a train as dark clouds pressed into her vision. She sighed and let go.

When she opened her eyes again, Derek was beside her, calling her name and caressing her cheek softly.

She didn't answer him because all at once her life was coming back to her. The fall had some-how released her memories. So many forgotten

moments were flowing back into her conscious-
ness at a frightening speed.

Justin and Mason had captured her on
Tuesday night. She felt again the strange sensation
of Mason inside her head, controlling her
thoughts.

Mason had tried to steal her sense of self
and make her one of them. He had shown her a
menacing black shadow. The same one she had
seen in that other dimension with Catty.

She had felt mesmerized by the whirling dark
cloud, and when he had told her to go toward it,
she had wanted to even though part of her knew
if she did, she would lose herself forever.

But someone had torn her away from Mason
and she had run. She tried to recall who, but that
memory hadn't come back to her yet.

Mason's power had been strong and continued absorbing her memories even after she had
escaped. That was why she couldn't remember
until now all the hours spent running and hiding
with Justin and Mason on her trail. She had run
for miles, slipping into shadows and sprinting

down dark alleys. They had almost caught her once and she had fallen down an embankment to escape them. That was why she had so many bruises the next day. She had managed to get away, and finally she had lost them and scrambled up a tree next to the apartment where she lived now. The window had been unlocked, so she had gone inside and crashed.

Then she remembered Pete. That's how Justin and Mason had caught her. Pete had asked her to dance at Planet Bang. He had seemed like any guy her age, except for the way his hands had been all over her, uninvited. She had tried to break away from him, but before she could, Justin and Mason had grabbed her. She had been able to escape because Derek had come.

"Derek," she said with surprise. "You saved me."

"I didn't. I should have been able to catch you."

"No, Tuesday night." The memory shot through her. "You grabbed my hand and jerked me away from those guys."

And then she had run.

"Yeah, I was jealous of the way all three were dancing with you." There was still anger in his voice. "I didn't know they were your cousins." He paused. "Well, they're not your cousins, but you know what I mean."

Earlier on Tuesday a mysterious force had been directing her to run. The same voice that had guided her since that first night when she had escaped the murderers in her parents' home. That's why she had taken her backpack with her to Planet Bang. She had never intended to go back to Mary's house. But before she ran, she had wanted to see what it would feel like to be an ordinary kid, hanging out with guys her age.

"Derek." She called his name softly this time.

His lips were close to hers now. "Yes," he breathed.

Why not tell him the truth? She had gone to Planet Bang hoping to see him and had foolishly flirted with Michael Saratoga only because Derek had been dancing with another girl when she got there.

"Who was the girl with the long hair you were dancing with on Tuesday night?" she asked.

"Who? You mean, Sara?" He laughed. "That's my younger sister."

She lifted her arms and wrapped them around his neck. She had liked him from the moment she had met him Monday at school. No wonder he thought she had been acting weird on Wednesday when she couldn't even remember his name.

But other memories came to her now. Ones that filled her with sadness. She saw her mother, father, and sister. Tears burned into her eyes. Having her memories suddenly restored made it feel as if they had died all over again.

"You're crying." Derek pressed her against him and rubbed her back soothingly.

She remembered the way she had struggled through the woodlot that first night and finally found shelter in the trashed boxes behind a liquor store. She had fallen into a deep sleep and was awakened the next morning by the woman who owned the store.

That began her first foster placement. More than anything she had wanted a home. She had lived in so many different houses and towns. West Covina. Ontario. Long Beach. Wilmington. She had kept a key from each one. That's why there were so many on her key chain. She felt suddenly sorry for herself, sorry that she had lived like a stray.

"Tianna." Derek spoke softly. "Why do those guys want you so badly?"

The answer came to her with sudden force. They were trying to stop her from bringing back the lost goddess before the dark of the moon. Was that tonight?

"Can you see the moon out tonight?" she asked suddenly.

Derek chuckled. "I haven't really noticed."

"Try," she told him. "It's important." Justin and Mason didn't want her to make the three become four again. Now she remembered what she was supposed to do, but it still felt like a puzzle.

"How 'bout the window?" she asked.

"You want me to see if there's a moon?" His

shoes scraped on the cellar floor as he started to move.

"No. I'll climb up there and get us out."

"I don't know." She could feel him shake his head. "The window looks like it hasn't been opened in a zillion years."

"It'll open for me." She stood and had started to walk to the wall under the window when an unexpected sense of doom struck her. What if she didn't survive the night? She turned abruptly and knocked into Derek. She wanted to know what a kiss felt like before she died.

"Derek, kiss me." Her heart was beating so hard, she was sure he could hear it.

"I've wanted to kiss you since the day I first saw you," he admitted. His hands caressed her shoulders, then glided down her back and pulled her closer to him.

"Then do it," she urged and rushed her tongue over her lips so they wouldn't be dry.

He leaned over her.and cradled her against him. She was aware of the warmth of his body.

Then his lips touched hers. The feeling startled her and she took in a sharp breath.

"It's your first kiss." His lips spoke against her ear.

"No——" she began. "Yes."

He brushed her hair back with his fingers as if she were fragile and precious, then he took her hands off his chest and placed them around his neck. He wrapped his own hands around her waist and kissed her again for a long time.

"Thank you." She sighed when he finally pulled away. "Now I have to rescue you."

"Because I kiss so good," he teased.

"That and because I got you into this mess in the first place."

They walked over to the wall beneath the window, holding hands.

"I'll climb up, then open the window," she ordered. "As soon as I'm outside, you follow."

She could feel his skepticism before he even spoke. "I don't know. That window looks like it's frozen shut. You'll never get it open."

"Trust me," she answered, and didn't bother to

hide her annoyance. "Just because I'm a girl . . ."

"I didn't say because you're a girl," he corrected her. "I said the window looks frozen shut. Some things are impossible."

"Nothing's impossible," she said. "Just watch me."

She touched the wall. It was covered with a slimy growth. Years of leaking water and damp earth had created a garden of fungus and mold over it. The smell was so strong, she could almost taste it on her tongue.

She focused her mind on moving the first brick out just a few inches so her toe had something to perch on, then she reached as high as she could and willed the brick beneath her palm away from the wall as well. She stepped on it, and felt the wall slump. Mud oozed from a crack, pushing out the mortar, and covered her foot.

"What's that sound?" Derek asked.

"The foundation is unstable," she explained. "From the water. I think there's a river of mud behind the bricks."

"We'd better hurry, then."

This time she used her telekinetic powers to move the brick more cautiously. A grinding sound filled the cellar as it scraped out a few inches.

Derek stood next to her, his hands on the wall, as if he were trying to hold back the flood of slimy soil. "Hurry," he repeated.

"So you believe I can do it now?" she asked, trying to make her voice come out teasingly, but her words sounded strained and filled with fear.

"I know you can," he encouraged.

She hadn't counted on the bricks being so old and the mortar decaying. She climbed up two more steps, then glanced at the window. She willed it open.

The frame protested with a shudder, then screeched against the side jambs as rusted hinges slowly pulled the window up.

"How'd you do that?" Derek asked. "You're not even close enough to reach it."

"I was," she argued. "You must have looked away."

"But even if you stretched, you couldn't touch it now."

"I was closer and I slipped," she said, exasperated. "Do we have to discuss it now? Just climb."

"But—"

She cut him off. "Justin and Mason could come back after us any minute."

"All right."

She took a deep breath and perched her toe on another brick, then pulled herself up and grabbed onto the windowsill. She struggled and wiggled into thick gluey spiderwebs. The cobwebs stuck to her face, and the more she wiped at them, the more they seemed to cling to her cheeks.

"What now?" Derek asked from below.

She didn't answer but rolled outside under a hibiscus bush. Low-hanging branches scratched at her back. She wiped her hands on the grass, then turned and looked back into the basement. She couldn't see a thing. "Can you feel the protruding bricks?"

Derek patted his hands along the wall, making a wet slick sound. "It feels like grabbing a handful of slime," he muttered.

"Thanks for sharing that," she whispered back. "I already cleared part of it away, and you won't even have to deal with the spiderwebs." She stretched over the windowsill to guide Derek. She could feel the bricks shift beneath her.

"This might not work," Derek said. "I'm heavier than you are by maybe thirty pounds. That would make a difference. It's like the whole thing is ready to collapse. Maybe you should just run for help."

"And leave you? No way. Try again."

This time as he started up, she used her power to force the bricks to stay.

He grasped a brick and pulled himself up. The foundation seemed to hold. "I can't believe it," he said with bafflement in his voice.

She felt her strength wavering, as if she was losing control. She wondered if there was a limit to her power. She focused until her forehead ached.

"Tianna," Derek called from below her. "I think we have a problem."

"What now?" she rasped, not hiding the exasperation in her voice. She could see the dim outline of his head. He only had a little way to go. She leaned in farther.

The marshy soil was sweeping through the bricks with a squishing sound. The odor was nauseating.

She concentrated, not sure if she had enough strength left to suppress the cave-in.

Silence followed.

"Start again," she said as a spider scurried over her face on feathery feet. When she turned to brush it away, she saw Mason and Justin. They were leaning against the front corner of the house about fifteen feet away, near the porch light, smoking cigarettes and talking.

CHAPTER TWENTY-ONE

"JUSTIN AND MASON are right out here," Tianna whispered down to Derek. "Be quiet."

"That's kind of hard to do with these bricks," he answered with frustration. His hand clutched the windowsill, and she rolled back to give him room to climb outside.

As he pulled himself through, her mental hold gave way. The sludgy mess of bricks and mud collapsed, emitting putrid smells of wet, brackish earth and decay.

She looked at Derek with complete surprise. "It hardly made any noise."

"There must have been so much mud that it insulated the sound of the bricks falling." Derek wiped his hands in the grass to get rid of the mud, then peered under the bobbing branches of the hibiscus to where Mason and Justin stood. "They didn't hear anything, at least. Maybe because of the traffic sounds."

Tianna listened. They were near a freeway or highway. The constant roar from cars and trucks could mask almost any sound.

"Now let's just hope the house doesn't collapse." New worry stirred inside her, but the frame of the house looked solid.

"Yeah," Derek agreed, and his hand went protectively to her back. "And hope they don't see us."

"Too late." Tianna cursed under her breath.

Mason and Justin threw away their cigarettes and started to walk toward them. The red embers made twin arches as they flew across the night sky.

"They're coming." She had grabbed Derek's arm, ready to run, when a resounding boom like distant thunder made her stop. "What's that?"

A '57 Chevy with dual exhaust pipes rumbled into the drive, its fenders ablaze with red and yellow metallic flames. It skidded sideways to a stop, the motor died, and Pete stepped out, dressed like a hipster in khakis, a white T-shirt, and an Armani jacket. Other than his clothes, he looked the same as he had when he had asked her to dance at Planet Bang. Then he turned and his face caught the porch light. She shuddered. His eyes had an unnatural glow.

Mason and Justin continued walking toward the car. They spoke in loud voices now, as if they were boasting. Pete whooped. The howl of his laughter made her skin crawl.

"They're pretty freaky guys," Derek said, as if he had felt the same shiver.

Then all three turned and strolled toward the front of the house. Under the harsh glare of the porch light Justin and Mason no longer looked young but cadaverous and wan. She wondered how old they really were.

"What are they?" Derek asked, as if he had also seen the hideous change in their faces.

As soon as the door closed, she took Derek's hand. "Now's our chance."

They scrambled out from under the hibiscus bush, then ran across the lawn toward a long line of eucalyptus trees.

"Go toward the traffic sounds." Derek indicated with his head.

"Where are we?" Tianna asked.

Derek took a deep breath. "It's got to be somewhere near the beach. You can smell the salt air."

They stepped over a bed of dried eucalyptus leaves, then slid down an embankment until they were on a busy street nestled against the beach. Derek pointed to a road sign. "Pacific Coast Highway," he read.

"But where?" she asked. "PCH runs up and down the entire California coast."

He shrugged. "We'll worry about that later. Let's go."

They ran along the shoulder of the road toward the bright headlights of the oncoming traffic. Their clothes flapped and their hair blew about their faces as air currents from the speeding cars breezed around them.

Soon they were at a strip mall. The smells of garlic and lemon came from a small Italian restaurant that had eight-by-ten glossies of celebrities on the wall.

"We can slow down now," Derek assured her, and let go of her hand. He wrapped his arm around her, and they strolled down the sidewalk. "We're on the strand and they're not likely to bother us here."

She wished she could feel so sure. She tried to steady her breathing as they walked past a long line of stores selling souvenirs. Sunburned kids, surfers, bikers, and tourists pushed through the stores, eating churros and hot dogs on sticks.

They had started to pass a pricey hotel with twenty-four-hour armed security guards when Derek clutched her hand and pulled her down a delivery driveway that curved behind the building.

"Why are we going here?" she asked, and started to go back. "It's a dead end."

"I got an idea." He smiled broadly.

Men were wheeling crates of vegetables from the bed of a truck onto the loading dock. Derek climbed onto the dock, then walked over to one of the men. She wondered if he was begging for something to eat.

In a few minutes he came back to her. "They're going to give us a ride back to L.A."

"Thanks." She rested her head against his chest. She liked him a lot, and that was precisely why she couldn't see him again. She had to find a way to tell him they couldn't hang out. It was too dangerous. She sighed. It was going to be hard. She loved the way he made her feel, but she couldn't think only about herself. Besides, he was probably searching for an excuse to break up with her right now. No guy wants a girl who has monstrous humanlike creatures chasing her down.

"Come on," Derek said, and they hurried onto the loading dock, then into the bed of the truck. They sat next to the cab on lettuce leaves, bits of broccoli, and carrot tops that had fallen from the crates.

She looked into Derek's deep blue eyes and wished she didn't have to tell him good-bye.

The driver closed the tailgate and gave them a thumbs-up and a big smile. In moments they were rolling up the driveway and onto the coast highway toward Los Angeles. Tears blurred her vision, making the traffic lights and taillights smear together into one reddish glow.

She took a deep breath, turned to Derek, and started to speak, but before she could say anything, he broke the silence. "I really like hanging out with you, Tianna."

"What?" She wiped her eyes. "After tonight I thought you'd never want to see me again."

"Are you kidding?" He seemed as surprised as she felt. "I've never had such an exciting night."

"Are you making fun of me?"

He shook his head. "From the first moment I met you, I knew you were the kind of girl who went running off the high dive into the deep end of the pool before you even knew how to swim."

She laughed.

He pulled her closer to him. "I like that rush of adrenaline I felt tonight."

The truck turned with a swerve in the road and she slid closer to him. She didn't move away.

"My adventures before have always been from reading books. I mean, look at me, Tianna."

She did. What did he have to complain about? His life seemed so perfect. Everyone at school liked him. He had tons of friends, and he got good grades.

"What about you?" she asked finally.

"I'm the only guy in the high school whose mother refused to sign a permission slip so I could play football. She said it was too dangerous. You can't believe the things I'm not allowed to do. Do you know that when I go snowboarding with Michael, I have to lie to my mother and tell her I'm going to visit his grandmother in Pomona?"

Tianna felt a sudden pang of jealousy. She wished she had a mother who cared about keeping her safe. "It's just that she loves you. That's the way she expresses it."

"Sure." He nodded. "But I have an adventurer's spirit," he went on. "More than anything I want to live a life like the one you showed me tonight."

Suddenly she felt annoyed. "It seems like fun to you because you've only had to deal with Mason and Justin for one night and now you can go home to your safe bed and remember all of this like a dream. But if you were always on the run from them, I can guarantee it wouldn't seem so great—" She stopped. How could she ever make him understand? "It's really unsafe for you to hang around with me. They're not going to stop until they destroy me, and they don't care who they take with me."

He put his arms around her. "How long have they been after you?"

"A long time," she answered, but she didn't elaborate. She didn't want his pity.

He held her tightly. "We've got to do something to stop them, then. Let's go to the police."

"I've tried that," she answered. "They don't believe me."

"Then we'll capture them ourselves and take them to the cops. They'll have to believe us if they see them."

"It's not that easy." She shook her head. "They have powers you don't understand."

"But we have to find a way to stop them so you don't have to be on the run. Then you could stay here and go to La Brea High." He kissed her temple. "That's what I want. I hope you do, too."

"More than anything," she murmured, but she had to face reality. It wasn't likely she was going to be able to do that.

The truck jerked to a halt. Derek tapped on the cab window and mouthed a thank-you to the driver, then they climbed over the tailgate and jumped off.

"We're only a block from my apartment." She started walking.

When they reached the stairs, she turned and faced him. "We're safe for right now. Let's get some rest and then tomorrow we'll make a plan." She looked at him and hoped he couldn't tell she was lying. She was going to leave Los Angeles tonight. Maybe go to Seattle. She didn't think she could pull Catty back from that other realm, and the longer she stayed here, the more she put the people she cared about in jeopardy.

"I'll pick you up first thing in the morning," he promised.

"Sure." She looked at him and wondered why now more than ever she didn't want to say good-bye.

"I really like you, Tianna." He tentatively slipped his hands around her waist, then bent closer as if he were going to kiss her.

She pulled abruptly away, afraid that his kiss would destroy her resolve. She turned, and as she hurried up the steps, she glanced at the night sky. The moon, only the thinnest crescent, was now a reminder that she had failed. Tomorrow night would bring the new moon and it would be too late.

"Tianna," Derek called. "What's wrong?"

She glanced back at him as she opened the door. She hated herself for the wounded look on his face. "I'll see you in the morning," she said.

CHAPTER TWENTY-TWO

BACK IN THE SMALL apartment, Tianna washed her hands, neck, and face, then glanced at her skirt. It was torn and covered with a black moldy mess from the cellar walls. She seemed to have a knack for destroying, clothes. She wanted nothing more than to take a hot shower and to slip into bed. She had started toward the bathroom, nerves throbbing, feet sore, when she caught something from the corner of her eye. She whipped around.

It looked like a huge swarm of gnats in the corner near the sink. She watched in wonder as the swirling cloud became denser and the dots seemed to come together and take form. Then Serena, Jimena, and Vanessa became visible in front of her.

She stumbled back, astonished. "You really are witches," she exclaimed, but she didn't feel afraid of them; she felt awestruck.

"We had to do something drastic to make you believe us," Serena said. "Because we need your help."

Tianna took another step away from them. "Look, if witchcraft is your thing, it's okay with me, but really I'm not into magic or spells."

They laughed as if she had said something funny.

Serena stepped forward. "You move objects with your mind and go into other dimensions, but you don't believe in magic. You are magic."

"How do you know that's what I do?" Tianna felt even more amazed than she had the moment before.

"Because we each have a power like yours." Vanessa pulled out one of the chairs from the table and sat down.

"But I'm not a sorceress," Tianna retorted. "I don't work any magic, and I can't cast spells. If I could, my life wouldn't be such a mess."

"I read minds," Serena confessed. "That's my gift, and I've gone inside your head. I know what you can do."

Tianna felt lost in wonder, but she believed Serena. That explained how she had figured out where she lived and how they had known that she and Corrine had been talking about Catty. "But how did you get here?" Tianna fell down in the chair opposite Vanessa. "Was it some kind of teleportation?" She was ready to believe anything now.

"No, we used my power," Vanessa explained. "I can make my molecules expand until I'm invisible. We waited outside until we saw you come back with Derek, then I made us all invisible so we could follow you inside."

Then Serena took Tianna's hand. "We're on

the side of good, like you. We battle the Atrox. That's what you've been running from, but you didn't even know it."

"Atrox?" Tianna shook her head. "I've never heard of it."

"It's an ancient evil," Jimena put in. "And Justin and Mason are two of its Followers."

"You know about them, too?" Tianna asked, stunned. "But how do you know? If you're not witches, then what are you?"

"Let me explain," Vanessa started. "In ancient times, when Pandora's box was opened—"

"Pandora?" Tianna laughed. "Don't tell me that myth is true."

Jimena nodded solemnly.

Then Serena continued, "The last thing to leave the box was hope—"

Tianna interrupted her. "I know the story."

"But there's more," Vanessa cautioned. "Listen."

Serena continued. "Selene, the goddess of the moon—"

"She's real, too?" Tianna knew at once that

Selene was the mysterious force who had directed her to run. That also explained why her internal guide was strongest during the full moon and weakest during the dark of the moon.

"Selene saw the creature that had been sent by the Atrox to devour hope," Serena said. "She took pity on the people of earth and gave her daughters, like guardian angels, to guard hope. We're those daughters. We're goddesses."

"Goddesses?" Tianna answered with a mocking grin, but this time when she looked at them, their faces seemed to glow.

You know what I'm saying is true, Serena breathed into her mind.

Tianna's derisive smile fell from her face. Serena had been able to speak to her by using her mind. The same way Justin and Mason could go inside her head. She felt staggered by everything they had told her, but even as stunning as it was, she believed them. Too may things had happened in her life for her not to.

"We need your help." Jimena's black eyes stared at her.

"What can I possibly do?" Tianna wondered aloud.

"Help us get Catty back," Vanessa urged.

"Catty was a goddess, too, wasn't she?" Tianna suddenly understood. "The three I'm supposed to make four again. I was supposed to bring Catty back to you."

"We hope you can," Vanessa coaxed. "Jimena had a premonition. That's her gift. We need to know if it's come true. Have you made contact with Catty already?"

"Yes. I think it was Catty, but the girl didn't wear a moon amulet like you three do."

"That's because hers exploded the night she disappeared," Serena explained.

"Can you contact her again?" Vanessa asked eagerly.

"The Atrox and its Followers have sworn to destroy the Daughters of the Moon because once we're gone, they will succeed," Serena put in. "Catty vanished when we were fighting a powerful member of the Atrox's inner circle. Our powers are weakened now that she's gone."

"But that's not the only reason we want her back," Vanessa added. "She was my best friend, and I miss her too much."

"But I tried already, and I couldn't bring her back," Tianna explained. "She's in a different dimension."

"How did you get there?" Vanessa asked.

"I was using my telekinetic powers and—"

Serena interrupted. "Can you try again and take us there?"

"I can go there, but I don't know how to get back," Tianna explained. "Twice I've gone, and both times I've only been able to return because someone on this side pulled me back."

Suddenly they all clasped onto her and she knew she had no choice.

"Take us," Jimena ordered.

"It's too dangerous," Tianna argued. "I don't know how to get back. Maybe I should practice a few times with just one of you."

"We'll figure out a way to get back once we're there," Vanessa said. "We have to get Catty. The dark of the moon starts tomorrow night, and then it will be too late. If we don't get her back tonight, she'll be a sacrifice."

Serena smiled. "We're willing to take the risk. All of us together will find a way back."

"I'll try." Tianna narrowed her eyes in concentration and pushed with her mind against the dresser. The wood warped and her vision blurred. She felt the girls' fingers gripping tighter and knew they had also experienced the change. Then the walls of the small apartment furrowed and became ridged as if she were looking at them through wavy glass. At last the glass shattered, reality fell away, and they stepped into that other realm.

"Wow." Vanessa sighed. "It's like being in the middle of an endless desert."

"Something's wrong," Tianna cautioned. "Don't let go of me." Her eyes darted around the strange gloom. She had an overpowering sense of danger.

"This is where you found Catty?" Vanessa asked, and stepped away from her.

"Yes. She's usually floating in some sort of

cloud." Tianna tried to hold on to Serena and Jimena, but already she could feel them pulling away. "Don't!" She tried to stop them, but it was too late.

"Don't worry so much." Suddenly Serena dove away from her, swimming through the curious air that was as buoyant as water.

Tianna looked at them. Maybe the only danger was in her mind. They didn't seem concerned, but instinct told her something was terribly wrong, and she always trusted that inner voice. "It doesn't feel right."

"What do you mean?" Jimena flapped her arms and a capricious smile crept across her face. *"Estoy volando. Mírame."*

"Don't go so far from me." Tianna wondered what had happened to them. It was as if they had forgotten the reason they had come here. She tried to keep her mind centered, but she could feel something seeping into her brain, trying to tranquilize her. Was someone manipulating their thoughts so they couldn't feel the danger hovering in the air? Tianna shuddered as realization took hold. The Atrox had used her to set a trap. The girls were going farther and farther from her, lured by a false sense of safety and euphoria.

"Come back!" she yelled, and her voice echoed around her in a taunting tone.

"Come on and join us, Tianna." Serena did a somersault like an underwater swimmer. "This is so cool."

"Your moon amulet," Tianna called back. "It changed colors. What does that mean?"

The amulet hanging around Serena's neck was shimmering with light. She glanced at Vanessa and Jimena; both their amulets were also glowing.

Tianna jumped, caught Jimena's arm, and jerked hard. "We have to go back," she said.

Jimena blinked suddenly as if she had snapped back from a dreamlike state. She looked at Tianna, then glanced down at her fiery amulet and understood immediately. "*¡Oye!*" she shouted. "Serena! Vanessa! Come back!"

Vanessa and Serena continued frolicking. Tianna watched in panic as the black mist began spilling into the air.

"The Atrox," Jimena breathed. "Get us out now."

"I told you I don't know how," Tianna said with panic.

"Then just do what you do to get in," Jimena said. "I'll get Serena and Vanessa." Jimena dove up into the air and jetted away as billowing shadows gathered over Tianna.

She narrowed her eyes in concentration, trying to penetrate the veil that divided the worlds.

Suddenly the shadow charged toward her. It hit her with the strength of a fist. She staggered back, then tripped and fell. The black vapor whipped around her.

She steadied herself and concentrated, using the full force of her mind to leave this realm. Her eyes went out of focus, and suddenly she was back in reality. She hit the side of the cupboard in the small apartment and fell, then sat up with a gasp.

"We did it," she yelled with excitement, and looked around the room. She was the only one who had made it back. Had she accidentally trapped the others?

A loud rap on the door made relief flood through her. Maybe they had come back and landed in another location, the same way Derek had found her running outside the apartment this morning.

She hurried to the door and swung it open. "Derek?"

Derek had an odd look on his face, and then she glanced behind him. Justin and Mason were there.

CHAPTER TWENTY-THREE

TIANNA AND DEREK stood on the cliff above a public beach, Mason and Justin beside them. A fog bank sat offshore, seeming to sweep in closer with each rising swell. The phosphorescent breakers tossed spray as they crashed over the rocks below, and distant lights on a pier reflected off the black water.

Mason stared at Tianna. "I didn't need to bring you here, Tianna," he said. "You already failed."

Justin snickered.

"But with you it's personal," Mason explained. "You made me look like a fool too many times."

Tianna glanced at the sky. "I still see a sliver of moon," she said.

That made them both laugh. "You think you can do something now, when we have all the goddesses?" Justin asked.

"Down the cliff," Mason ordered.

Tianna looked at the edge. "Where?"

"A path over there." Justin shoved her back. "And don't try to use your fancy mind stuff because you don't want anything to happen to Derek."

She nodded and started down the path.

"I'm sorry," Derek whispered behind her. "I wanted to play the big hero, so I went back to Planet Bang to get my car and they found me there."

She smiled ruefully at him.

Derek sighed. "They got your address by going through my mind."

"Thanks, Derek!" Mason laughed.

Tianna pushed through the chaparral and walked cautiously over the jagged rocks. Because it was almost a new moon, the tide was at its lowest, and she sloshed through a small tide pool that normally would have been much deeper, then stepped onto wet sand where a wave had left bubbling foam. Another wave hit her ankles with a shock of cold. When the water receded, she felt tingling on the soles of her feet from tiny mole crabs burrowing back into the soupy sand.

Fires down the beach caught her eye.

"Toward the light," Justin ordered.

She tottered in the sand and walked around a tangled bed of kelp, then headed up the shore with an increasing sense of doom. As she got closer, she saw that the fires were actually torches set in the sand. The flames at the end of the long poles waggled in the ever present wind, the tips radiating an uncanny whiteness that seemed different from any fire she had seen before. Ice-blue sparks spit into the cold night air and continued to glow until they spun out of sight. The fires were breathtaking and left a slight odor of sulfur in the air.

Followers standing on the beach looked at her with hunger, as if they had waited for Tianna a long time. Suddenly, she realized why they wanted her. With her gone, there was no chance that the four goddesses could ever be united again.

She glanced into Justin's eyes as he took off his shirt and stood under the first torch. The flame flapped and the standing goat tattooed on his arm seemed to move.

She stopped, startled by the tattoo. There was something familiar about the shape, and then she knew. She had seen it on the arm of the men who had stolen into her home when she was a little girl. She glanced up and Justin understood her look.

"So you remember now," he said with a smirk.

She nodded. She felt weak and powerless. The same way she had felt that night so many years back when they had invaded her house. She wondered what they had wanted with her even then that could have made them commit such an atrocity.

"Sit," Mason ordered.

She collapsed onto the sand with a childish desire to cry.

Derek sat beside her. "Tianna, what's going on?"

"Some ceremony. I don't know. I guess they're getting ready to cross us over."

"Who are the goddesses they kept talking about?" he asked.

"I'll explain later," she hushed him.

"Later?" he exclaimed. "You think we're going to survive this?"

"I am," she said with determination. "And I'll save you."

"Right," he scoffed. Then he looked at her with his deep blue eyes. "You know, Tianna, I think we're going to die, so if you know, then it's only fair you tell me."

Tianna looked at him. "You're right. I can tell you what I know, but that doesn't mean it's going to make sense because it still isn't clear to me. Most of it I just learned myself about an hour ago."

She started to explain as more Followers arrived at the beach. They didn't look like kids coming to the beach for a picnic. Some guys wore tuxedos, others stepped out in painted and patched jeans, but all looked glamorous.

Tianna continued telling Derek everything that had happened. He seemed to accept all that she said. She told him about accidentally trapping Jimena, Vanessa, and Serena when they tried to rescue Catty.

"So now instead of saving one goddess and making the Daughters of the Moon four again, I actually lost all of them." She finished.

"Space is a funny thing," Derek mused.

"That's not exactly the reaction I expected."

"The universe is constructed of atoms," he continued.

"Derek, I know that, and I really don't feel like talking about science in my last moments on earth. Can't you think of some way to get us out of this?"

He grinned and went on, "Spaces exist between these atoms, and within these spaces are other atoms that create a parallel universe, one existing simultaneously with ours."

"Okay." She smiled. "Now you've got my attention."

"That other realm and this one are woven together," Derek said.

"So," Tianna concluded, "if Vanessa, Jimena, and Serena are being held captive in another dimension and if the ceremony is going to take place on this beach, then they're probably right here behind the veil that divides the worlds."

"That would be my guess." He nodded. "Now do something."

"Say no more." Tianna leaned over and kissed his cheek quickly. "Don't forget to pull me back like you did this morning when you saw me running, wrapped in the bedsheet."

His eyes sparkled as if he enjoyed that memory. "I'm ready," he announced, and glanced at his watch. "Five minutes is all I'll give you, then I'm going to yank hard."

"That's all I need," she agreed. "Either they're there or they aren't."

She gazed at the fires and narrowed her eyes in total concentration.

CHAPTER TWENTY-FOUR

THE FLAMES ON THE torches trembled, and then it was as if she were looking at the ocean through a crumpled sheet of plastic. The roar of the surf became distant, and at that moment the membrane dividing the two worlds rippled and swelled before bursting.

She found herself standing in that other realm. It was eerily still and a strange gentle radiance filled the air, although she couldn't see the source.

"Vanessa," she called. "Serena. Jimena. Can you hear me?"

Then she felt a change in the air and looked cautiously behind her, sensing something evil hidden in the gray nothingness. She cursed silently and called their names again.

Where were they? Derek's explanation had seemed so reasonable. She had been confident she would find them here. She had expected to see all four of them tied up together. Now she wondered if she had walked into another trap. Maybe this was even part of the ceremony.

She had taken only a few steps when she had to stop. She realized with a grateful sigh that Derek had taken her hand and was keeping her bound to the real world.

A soft fluttering sound made her look around. "Hello," she called. "Is someone there?" Her words fell into the air with a tremor of fear.

A flapping noise made her look up. Jimena waved and dove toward her.

"You did it!" she yelled. "I knew you'd find a way to get us back."

"I almost didn't." Tianna spoke softly. "And we're not safe yet. I still have to get us out."

"What is this place?" Vanessa yelled as she soared into view. "It's like being in a huge tank of water without the water."

"Another dimension." Tianna shrugged. "Where are Serena and Catty? We don't have much time." How many minutes had gone by already?

Catty and Serena appeared from a roiling mist. Serena was pulling Catty by her arm.

"This is Tianna," Vanessa said to Catty. "The one who first saw you in a séance."

"It wasn't really a séance," Catty insisted. She still seemed weak, but not as weak as the last time Tianna had seen her. "And how do you know she's not one of them? After all, she trapped you in here with me."

"She's not," Serena insisted. "I told you, Followers killed her parents." Then she glanced at Tianna. Her eyes seemed worried that what she had said might upset her. "Sorry, I read it in your mind back in your apartment."

"How did you know they were Followers?" Tianna asked. "I didn't even know until just a few minutes ago."

"I recognized the tattoo," Serena explained.

Jimena took Vanessa's hand. "She's going to get us out of here. Hold on."

As they joined hands, Tianna had an uneasy feeling. It was as if the mysterious force were alerting her to danger again. She glanced around, wondering if that deadly shadow were about to filter into the air.

"What's wrong?" Serena asked.

"It shouldn't be this simple," Tianna answered. "Why did the Atrox trap you only to let you go so easily? I'm starting to get a weird feeling. I always trust my instincts, and something's telling me this isn't right."

"Why does everything have to be hard?" Vanessa asked. "Maybe for once we're getting a break."

"It never works that way," Jimena answered.

Tianna felt a tug on her hand. "We're going back," she said. She had forgotten that Derek had agreed to pull her back in five minutes no matter what.

Suddenly they were sprawled in the cold, foaming surf.

Derek yelled, "Look out!"

The Followers bolted toward them, kicking up sand. There was nowhere to go but back into the other dimension. Even the ocean seemed too forbidding. The high tide had now started to come in.

"What are we going to do?" Tianna said.

"Stay and fight." Jimena laughed dangerously as the Followers slowly circled them.

Justin took a step forward, his eyes glowing. The Followers crowded beside him

"We're outnumbered." Tianna realized now she had made another foolish mistake. "Maybe we should go back to the other side."

"No way," Serena argued.

"Not a chance." Catty looked strong again now that she was back in the real world.

Tianna wondered what they were doing. They didn't seem afraid. Didn't they understand how dangerous these guys could be? Instead they stood together, their amulets glowing, and a golden aura wavered around them, coloring the beach with inexplicable rainbow lights. Then their eyes seemed to dilate as if energy were building inside their heads.

"They look like the guys from Zahi's old group," Catty said with disgust in her voice.

"You're right," Serena agreed.

Tianna stood motionless. "You've fought them before?"

"We tried to tell you," Vanessa said.

Their eyes flashed with anticipation.

Tianna wondered why they seemed so eager to fight. There were too many Followers, and before she could even start to consider how many, Mason stepped forward with a twisted grin on his bony face.

"We have never fought so many at one time before." Jimena looked directly at Mason. "It's been something we've been wanting to do for a long time."

Mason raised an eyebrow. "You won't win."

Suddenly Jimena, Catty, Vanessa, and Serena locked arms, and the air around them glowed, then pulsed and rushed toward Mason with amazing force. He staggered back.

"Justin," he called. "Time to show them the strength of the Atrox."

"I hear you." Justin stepped next to him.

This time when the girls sent an attack, Mason and Justin pushed it back. The force exploded in electrical waves around Serena and Jimena. Their moon amulets sparkled, then glowed weaker. Tianna could feel something happening.

She glanced back at Justin.

"Serena," Tianna yelled too late. Justin attacked. Even at this distance she could feel the heat of his power.

Small fires bobbed on the surf before going out and the dry chaparral smoldered.

Then Jimena and Serena leaned together and Catty and Vanessa joined them, all four locked arms again, and their power crackled across the night.

Justin deflected their hit, sending sparks like a million fireflies swirling up and around.

Tianna felt spellbound by what she had seen. Derek grabbed her shoulders and pulled her back.

"You're too close," he cautioned. "Can you believe this?"

"I don't think they're winning," Tianna said, worried.

The air smelled of ozone, smoke, and sulfur. She stared at Mason through the shower of embers. A strange light covered his face, and then she realized it was coming from the moon amulets. His eyes flashed with evil anticipation, as if he enjoyed the fight. The others Followers gathered close around him, with the same hungry look in their eyes.

She moved in front of Derek, ready to protect him but not sure how.

"For the first time," Justin said, "all four goddesses will join the Atrox at once. Think what that will do to the world."

The others pushed forward.

Tianna was doubtful the Daughters could

fight so many by themselves, and she didn't understand her fierce need to protect Derek. Then an idea came to her. She had already made the three four again. Her mission was accomplished. Why not just take Derek and flee?

"Come on." Tianna grabbed Derek's hand and started to pull him toward the jagged rocks.

"Where?" he asked, eyes wide.

"Back to the road." She motioned with her head. "It's not our fight."

They scrabbled up the rocky cliff.

She heard Jimena, Serena, Vanessa, and Catty reciting an incantation or prayer. *"O Mater Luna, Regina nocis, adiuvo me nunc."* They chanted the words over and over.

Justin scoffed. "Look at the moon tonight, goddesses. It's only a crescent, soon to disappear. The queen of the night won't help you now."

Tianna glanced back. The power emanating from Jimena, Catty, Serena, and Vanessa made the air waver and glow, but not as brightly as before. Their strength seemed to be fading.

Derek took her arm. "Do something."

"Me?" Tianna said in exasperation. "I don't have the kind of powers they have. The best I can do is save you."

The air rocked as Mason and Justin attacked again. Serena staggered back from their smashing blow, her moon amulet on fire. Jimena caught her.

"They're not going to be able to defeat them without your help," Derek insisted.

She turned to him. "But what can I do?"

CHAPTER TWENTY-FIVE

"USE YOUR POWER," Derek encouraged.

An idea came to her, and slowly she made her way back down to the rocks. Waves crashed over her. She stood on a boulder and concentrated until she had created a breeze. She made the wind swirl around her, and when it had enough momentum, she sent it charging down the beach. The tempest slashed through the sand and scooped it up, then whirled like a dust devil, surrounding the Followers.

They covered their eyes as the sandy winds screeched about them.

Justin stopped his attack.

Mason looked around, his baggy clothes flapping wildly as the squall circled him.

Then Justin caught her eyes, and in a flash she understood that he knew what she was doing. She felt him piercing her mind. His mental force throbbed through her, forcing her to stop. She could hear Derek say something, but his voice was too far away.

She tried to fight Justin with stubborn determination, but then Mason joined him. Their power was too strong, and her head ached until the pain became intolerable. She collapsed and released her power as they cut through her resistance.

The wind went out of control and blustered around the beach. It tore into her lungs, smothering her with air too thick to breathe. What had she done? She was going to destroy them all.

She grabbed onto a rock and pulled herself up. Sand scraped her face and arms, and the night turned an odd coppery dark. She squinted, eyes tearing from the grit, and held her hand over her nose and mouth while taking a stumbling step forward.

Sand gummed her mouth, coated her tongue, and clogged her nostrils. She spit and coughed. With laboring steps she continued up the cliff.

Then through the swirling whirlwind a hand grabbed her shoulder and pulled her onto an outcropping of jagged rock. The air was clearer there. She sneezed and brushed the sand from around her eyes.

She looked back at the strange roiling clouds below her.

"You did that." Derek looked down at the howling winds with amazement.

"I think I killed them all." She started to cry.

Then Jimena, Catty, Vanessa, and Serena pushed through the sandstorm and climbed on the rock.

"You did it!" Serena yelled, and spit sand from her mouth.

"You saved us." Vanessa hacked.

"I almost suffocated us all," Tianna argued.

"No, you didn't," Catty replied. "You still gave everyone a way to escape. It's just that the way the winds were blowing, the Followers had to run away from us down the beach."

"Yeah," Vanessa agreed. "Very smart."

Tianna smiled.

"Let's get away from here, anyway," Catty urged.

Vanessa hugged her, obviously glad to have Catty home.

They started up the cliff, brushing sand from their hair and ears.

"How did you get in that other dimension?" Tianna asked Catty when they were safely on the street and walking down the strand.

"Long story." Catty shook her head. "We were fighting this powerful Follower."

"And Catty got hit because she was trying to save me," Vanessa added. "She's such a good friend."

"So what happened?" Tianna asked.

"I saw that he was going to have a direct hit

on me," Catty explained. "So I tried to escape, but when I opened the tunnel—"

"That's Catty's gift," Vanessa interrupted. "She travels in time, and the tunnel is what she uses to get from one place to the next."

"His force hit me just as I opened the tunnel, and it threw me into that other dimension," Catty continued. "I figured I was going to be sacrificed at the next dark moon. So I was just as shocked as you were when I first saw you. I tried to warn you then."

"But you wrote 'Help me' on my wall," Tianna said, confused.

Catty shook her head. "The Followers wrote that. They were trying to lure you to stay. I'm the one who scratched 'stay away' because I knew it was too dangerous for you to rescue me."

Then all four turned as if they had suddenly become aware of Derek. "Should we fix his mind so he doesn't remember?" Serena asked.

"No." Tianna jumped in front of him. "Please don't. He loves adventure."

They all looked at her curiously.

"I'm not going to tell anyone," Derek promised. "If that's what you're worried about. No one would believe me, anyway."

That made them all laugh.

"Let's go home," Vanessa said.

Tianna sighed. More than anything she wanted to go home, but she didn't have a place to go. She walked slower and fell behind the others.

Derek took her arm. "What's wrong?"

She couldn't look at him.

"After what we've been through tonight, I can't believe you have a secret you're not going to tell me." He put a comforting arm around her.

She looked up. "I don't have a home to go to. I guess I can go to a shelter or the nearest police station."

He thought about it. "My older sister is away at college. I bet my mom would let you spend the night in her room."

Jimena was suddenly beside her. "You can stay with me. My *abuelita* would love to have someone living with her who hasn't heard all her stories."

"Or you could live with me," Vanessa offered

quickly. "We'll clear out the bedroom where my mom stores all her clothes. She could use another daughter as a model for her dress designs."

"We have room, too," Catty put in. "My mom will say yes to anything once she sees that I'm okay."

"See?" Vanessa said. "You have plenty of homes."

Tianna took a deep breath. "Thanks."

"But there's someplace we have to take you first," Serena said.

"Where?" Tianna asked, baffled.

"You'll see." Catty smiled mysteriously, then she glanced at Derek. "Sorry, Derek, this is one place you can't go."

"That's okay." Derek laughed. I've had enough adventure for one night. I'll catch a bus home."

He pulled Tianna away from the others and whispered against her cheek. "It looks like you're going to be staying in L.A. I'm glad."

"Me, too," she said and softly kissed him good night.

CHAPTER TWENTY-SIX

"**W**HERE ARE YOU taking me again?" Tianna asked suspiciously as they walked through the massive Cedars-Sinai complex. Nurses going off duty turned and stared at them, covered with sand and scrapes.

"Don't worry." Vanessa smiled. "You'll like it."

The fragrance of night-blooming jasmine filled the air as they stepped up to the entrance of a gray apartment building and Catty pressed a button on the security panel.

"Yes," a voice answered.

"It's Catty."

A loud hum opened the magnetic lock.

They entered and immediately caught their reflections in the mirrors and started laughing. Even though they had brushed at the sand, they were still covered with a fine layer of dust on their faces and arms. Their eyes were bloodshot, and their hair looked as if it had been moussed with Play-Doh. They continued laughing as they crowded onto the elevator and rode up to the fourth floor.

When the doors opened, they walked down a narrow outside hallway.

A woman wearing a white silky gown stood in the open door of her apartment. She was short, with long gray hair that curled thickly to her shoulders. "Look at you! Whatever happened?" She embraced Catty and hugged her tightly.

"Is that Catty's mother?" Tianna asked.

"No, this is Maggie," Serena replied.

Maggie smiled at Tianna. "So this is the friend you told me about." Her amiable eyes glanced over her, and then she motioned them to come inside.

Candles blazed, and the flames reflected in mirrors and gilded frames. It gave everything a fairy-tale feel.

"Why don't you each take a shower while the others talk," Maggie offered. "You'll find clean robes and towels, oils and soaps in the back bathroom."

Tianna was the first one to shower and dress in one of the silky robes. When she came out, Jimena went in.

"Come join us, please." Maggie offered her a chair and a cup of tea.

Tianna sat down as Serena, Vanessa, and Catty continued to tell Maggie all that had happened.

Finally they had all finished showering and sat together, hair wet and wrapped in towels. Maggie pulled out a moon amulet that matched the ones Serena, Jimena, and Vanessa wore. She handed it to Catty.

"You lost yours," she said simply.

Catty slipped it on. "Thanks." Immediately it turned an opalescent color and reflected the candle flames with multicolored sparks.

Then Maggie walked around the table until she stood behind Tianna. "And now, my dear, I have one for you, too."

"Me?" Tianna looked at her in disbelief.

Maggie clasped the amulet around Tianna's neck. The silver stone felt good on her skin and gave her comfort.

"Thanks." Tianna touched it. "It's pretty."

"It's more than style," Vanessa said.

"You'd better tell her, Maggie," Jimena coaxed.

Maggie moved a candle to the middle of the table and stared across the flame at Tianna, her blue eyes intense. "Selene has looked down and decided to make you a goddess because of the courage and fearlessness and the talent you have shown in using your telekinetic powers to fight evil."

Tianna laughed and held up her hands. "Does a goddess have cuts and bruises and ripped fingernails?"

Maggie nodded. "*Tu es dea, filia lunae.* You are a goddess, a Daughter of the Moon."

Tianna stopped laughing.

"We told her the story already," Serena put in.

"And about the Atrox, too," Vanessa added. "But I think that was a little harder for her to believe."

Maggie nodded. "The greatest strength of the Atrox is that people no longer believe that the demonic walk among us. So you see why it is so important that you help fight it."

"Me?" Tianna whispered.

Maggie nodded. "Catty, Vanessa, Jimena, and Serena have no choice. That is what they were born to do and it is my responsibility to guide them and to help them understand their powers. But you are being offered a choice."

Tianna felt happy. Since she had lost her family, she had wanted to belong somewhere.

"That mysterious voice that seemed like an inner guide," Tianna asked. "Was that Selene?"

Maggie nodded. "Selene was always guiding

you. She looked down on you that first night and felt pity for what the Followers had done and for what you were going to endure. And now because you have proved yourself, she is allowing you to become—"

"A goddess," Tianna whispered.

"A Daughter of the Moon." Maggie corrected her with a smile.

"But what about Justin and Mason?" Tianna wondered if she would always be on the run. "Will they still be after me?"

"No," Maggie assured her. "You have succeeded in fulfilling what you were meant to do. You brought the four Daughters of the Moon together again."

"And now we're five," Catty added.

"But why did they have to take my family from me?" Tianna asked.

"Evil doesn't have a rational explanation. I do know the Atrox sent them into the past to correct what it had seen happening in the future. But by altering the past, they actually created the future that was always meant to be."

Tianna looked down. "So the Atrox saw me saving Catty in the future and it sent Justin and Mason back into the past to destroy me."

"Yes," Maggie said. "Now all of you must go home. You have families who are worried about you."

Tianna looked down.

Maggie's soft hand cupped her chin. "You most of all, my dear. Mary and Shannon and Todd care about you very much. You need to go home at once and let them know you're all right."

"Home?" Tianna repeated the word so softly, she wasn't even sure she had said it aloud.

"Yes," Maggie answered. "I'll come with you, if you like."

Maggie and Tianna stood outside the large brick Tudor home. A line of smoke wafted from the massive chimney.

"I believe Mary is sitting up waiting for you," Maggie encouraged. "I'll wait here until you go inside."

"I'm nervous, " Tianna said. "What if the

things she said about me coming back were just talk? Maybe she doesn't really want me."

"She does," Maggie answered simply. "She lost all the family she had, and now she desperately needs you children."

Tianna looked up at the window, then took a deep breath and walked up to the house.

Mary answered the door tentatively, looking over Tianna's head, then up and down the street. "You're alone?"

"They're gone," Tianna said. "Can I stay here?"

In response, Mary smiled and opened the door wide. Tianna walked inside. Flames flickered in the hearth, and the smell of popcorn wrapped around her.

Shannon and Todd looked up in surprise when they saw her. Shannon ran to her with arms spread as wide as wings, and Todd did happy wheelies around the room.

Hours later, stomach filled with popcorn and Pepsi, Tianna crawled onto the soft cotton-flowered sheet and pulled the comforter over her head. Her bed smelled fresh and new, and she had a cozy feeling that she hadn't felt for a long time. Tears stung her eyes. She missed her parents and Jamie, but now at least she had a chance to start to live a normal life after so many years of running and living on the street.

She stared out the window at the dark night sky and touched the amulet hanging around her neck.

"Goddess," she murmured. The word felt so right.

Don't miss the next

DAUGHTERS OF THE MOON book,

moon Demon

"VANESSA!" MICHAEL SARATOGA waved at her. He wore a tight blue short-sleeved shirt and faded jeans with frayed hems and heavy black boots.

In moments he was next to her and putting his arm around her. She breathed in his clean, soapy smell. She liked him even more than she had when they had first started dating and now she wanted to take their relationship to another level.

His hand smoothed up her side as if he sensed what she was thinking.

Her heart raced, wondering if she should tell

him her secret desire now. Why not? They were alone. She cleared her throat and started to speak. "Michael, I want to talk to you about—"

He tilted his head and in the slant of sunlight she caught something in his eyes. They looked dark and tense.

"Is everything okay, Michael?"

"Sure. Why wouldn't it be?" he asked and the smile returned to his eyes.

Maybe it had only been a reflection of the sun. "You looked different. That's all."

"New haircut." He shrugged and absently brushed his free hand through his hair. She took a deep breath. She should just say it. She trusted Michael. She loved him. She'd never had such a crush on a guy before. She liked the way he looked at her, the way his lips curled around perfect white teeth when he smiled—the way he was now. What was it about him that made her feel so good?

"Have you decided what you want for your birthday yet?" Michael asked.

"Go out, I guess."

"I want the celebration to be special for you," he said. "Anything. You name it. I'll make it happen."

She bit her lip, trying to find the words to say what was on her mind. His hand reached over and cupped her cheek as if he sensed her turmoil.

"What?" he teased. "You only bite your lip when you have something important to say."

"I—" Her feet began to tingle. This was as bad as the first time he tried to kiss her. "I want to . . . I want you to . . ." She stopped. She felt heat rising to her cheeks. Any other guy wouldn't wait for his girlfriend to ask.

She cleared her throat and started again even though her legs had started to become a dusty swirl.

"Just say it." His gorgeous eyes never left hers. "I won't bite."

"I want . . ." Invisibility was too dangerously near. She couldn't ask the question now. She'd become a ghost right in front of him. "I want you to stop at the market on the way home so I can buy some Jelly Bellies."

He laughed. "Is that all? I don't know why you were so nervous to ask me that. I thought it was going to be something important." He seemed disappointed.

Vanessa stared off and wondered when she was going to get the nerve up to tell him what she really wanted.

LYNNE EWING is a screenwriter who also counsels troubled teens. In addition to writing all of the books in the Daughters of the Moon series, she is the author of two ALA Quick Picks: *Drive-By* and *Party Girl.* Ms. Ewing lives in Los Angeles, California.

Discover the secrets of the
DAUGHTERS OF THE MOON

DAUGHTERS OF THE MOON # 1
GODDESS OF THE NIGHT
0-7868-0653-2

DAUGHTERS OF THE MOON # 2
INTO THE COLD FIRE
0-7868-0654-0

DAUGHTERS OF THE MOON
NIGHT SHADE
0-7868-0708-3

DAUGHTERS OF THE MOON # 4
THE SECRET SCROLL
0-7868-0709-1

DAUGHTERS OF THE MOON # 5
THE SACRIFICE
0-7868-0706-7

DAUGHTERS OF THE MOON
THE LOST ONE
0-7868-0707-5

$9.99 Each (#$13.99 CAN)
Join the Adventure

AVAILABLE AT BOOKSTORES EVERYWHERE